GW00384610

Chapte

THE public thought of Mr. Justice Parlant as a character; those who came into professional contact with him added certain adjectives to such description. In Court he would wait with ill-hid impatience for the chance to make some typically witty remark, and if Counsel wished to retain any chance of winning their cases they laughed as loudly, and perhaps for a greater length of time, than the general public, who probably had not understood the reference anyway. Criminals took much care to try not to appear before him, some even going to the lengths of confining their criminal activities to circuits other than his. Mr. Justice Parlant thought that criminals should pay for their misdeeds and sentenced them accordingly, a philosophy that proved highly unpopular.

To a more restricted public the Judge was also known as an ardent collector of snuff-boxes. This collection was an extensive and comprehensive one, and contained many pieces that dealers or owners had originally valued at what they subsequently discovered was much too great a sum. One did not argue with the Judge about the price of a snuff-box, any more than one appealed to him for mercy.

Blackshirt liked snuff-boxes.

*

Richard Verrell carried the plates through to the kitchen where they would remain until the morning when Roberts would wash them. He then returned to the sitting-room, lay back in the comfort of his favourite arm-chair and lit a cigarette. He warmed the brandy glass in the palm of his hand, appreciated the bouquet, reflected that life was indeed a pleasant thing.

He thought about the Judge's house and mentally checked on which would be the best way of breaking in. He suddenly grinned. Should anything go wrong, and he be caught, he could be certain of one thing: Mr. Justice Parlant would try the case, and any recommendation for mercy would be treated with the contempt it deserved.

He sipped the cognac, picked up and began to read a book written by an author he knew. Without any sense of malice he came to the agreeable conclusion that the said author could not write.

The grandmother's clock struck, and he closed the book, stood up. It was time to change. The knowledge brought him pleasure and the first flush of welcome excitement, an excitement that never grew less, no matter how often Blackshirt set out to challenge the world.

Ten minutes later he was the cracksman, dressed in black shirt, trousers, coat; then he carefully knotted a white scarf about his neck and tucked the ends inside his dress coat, and no one would have thought him anyone but a man going out to a party or returning from one.

He walked the mile and a half to the Judge's home, entered the garden of the house on the right. There he stripped off the scarf, donned black gloves and hood, and became no more substantial than a shadow. He crossed from the one garden to the other, checked that all was quiet, entered the rather ugly building by way of the french windows.

The snuff-boxes were displayed in glass-fronted cabinets in a room on the first floor. They had been set out with much taste and formed an attractive collection: so much so, that Blackshirt decided to take no more than one box, and that as a memento and not according to its value. Since he did not have to steal to live, he did not do so when there was cause why he should not.

He took a glass-cutter from the belt of tools he wore about his waist and prepared to cut the glass front of one of the cabinets. He ran the diamond down the surface, realized that what had seemed an insecure housing for so valuable a collection was nothing of the sort: the glass was toughened by a new process which made it as strong as steel. He transferred his attention to the lock of the door, found that that, too, would not yield quickly.

Behind his hood, Blackshirt grinned. Had he succeeded too easily he would have felt cheated! A sentiment that Mr. Justice Parlant would have failed to understand.

He continued to try to force an entry, met with no success. The men who had made the cabinet had produced something that showed as much craftmanship as the works of gold and silver it housed.

*

The butler lay in his bed and tried not to think of the bottle of whisky that lay hidden in the top cupboard of the pantry. Had his wife not insisted earlier in the evening on remaining in the kitchen, from where she could

Double for Blackshirt

Roderic Jeffries

© Roderic Jeffries 1958

Roderic Jeffries has asserted his rights under the Copyright, Design and Patents Act, 1988, to be identified as the author of this work.

First published in 1958 by John Long Ltd.

This edition published in 2018 by Endeavour Media Ltd.

Table of Contents

see into the pantry, he would have been able to partake of his nightly drink; but she had, and since he had recently sworn never to touch the stuff again, he had had, perforce, to go without.

It seemed as though the liquid were slipping caressingly down his throat and for a brief second he found contentment; then the illusion was gone and his mouth became once more an arid desert.

Temptation of thought became too great, and, very daring, he slipped out of his side of the bed, ever heedful not to awaken his wife who would have, with her over-suspicious mind, decided she knew where he was going.

He left the bedroom and descended the stairs and there was joy within him. He would not have a very big drink, certainly nothing like the one that had necessitated his leaving his last place of employment, but it would be sufficient to ease the pain in his throat.

Since the old boy and his guests were asleep, the butler decided to risk walking through the library and the gun-room—as the place in which the snuff-boxes were kept was called for some quite illogical reason. He crossed the library, his rate of progress ever getting quicker as the source of pleasure neared, and with the whole of his mind occupied by innumerable bottles of whisky, opened the door of the gun-room.

'Come in,' said a cheerful voice.

For one happy moment he thought he must be drunk, then truth revealed that he was not. Shock flooded his system, and had not an exceedingly strong arm wrapped itself about his neck he would have fallen to the ground.

A torch was switched on and the light played quickly over his face and body. There was a short chuckle. 'Definitely not the athletic type.'

Blackshirt released his grip on the other, leaned against the nearest case, and waited.

The butler had never been in greater need of the consolation of whisky, and it was ironic that this should be at a time when there could be no hope of obtaining any. Indeed, for several moments his frightened mind was convinced that never again would his lips taste that delicious nectar; then, by the light of the torch, he made out the clothes the intruder was wearing. 'Blackshirt,' he muttered.

'Correct.'

The butler became more cheerful. It was said that provided the victim behaved himself the cracksman did not carve him into small pieces. The butler knew he would be the very model of decorous behaviour.

'Haven't got the keys, have you?' asked Blackshirt.

'What . . . what keys?'

'To this cabinet.'

'The master keeps them on his person, even when he retires to bed.'

'I could wake him up and ask for them,' suggested Blackshirt.

The butler imagined the effect such action would have on the Judge and all but smiled. It must be true that every cloud had its silver lining.

'Trouble is, that would be cheating.'

Blackshirt spoke seriously, strange as the words might seem. He was not in any immediate hurry, and thus to wake up the Judge and take the key from him would be to short-cut the challenge of the toughened glass and the recalcitrant lock. Naturally, had the butler had it on him, then not to use it would have been tempting fate, and no cracksman ever did that.

There was a short silence. Finally Blackshirt spoke. 'Will you sit down there and remain quite quiet?'

The butler did as requested.

'Since you're here, you might as well make yourself useful: hold the torch so that the lock is illuminated.'

The butler held the torch. He was not a man of courage, and was, therefore, happy to obey orders: reflection told him that, had he been courageous to the extreme, there was in the figure clothed in black that which would have restrained him. The cracksman might speak lightly, but no one could doubt that should he so wish he could change into a grim fighter, who would have to travel a great distance before he found an equal.

'Remarkably efficient lock,' said Blackshirt several moments later as he stepped back and rested.

'Best the Judge could obtain. The man who installed them all said they were guaranteed burglar-proof.'

'Did he?' The cracksman cut short his period of rest, returned to the task in hand. He inserted the pick into the lock once more, began to probe. He called the instrument a pick, but it was very much more than that. It was thin, made of the strongest steel, with one end curved slightly. When placed in position, it would force open the type of lock with which

Blackshirt was faced, merely through pressure, but the placing of the point had to be exact. An error of one hundredth of an inch meant failure.

'Are you going to take all the snuff-boxes?' asked the butler suddenly.

'Don't shout so loudly.'

'I was whispering,' he retorted.

'Try a lower key then,' replied Blackshirt, to whom the words had sounded like a bugle call.

The butler was silent, rightly feeling he had been severely rebuked. Annoyed, he told himself that honest men were not required to be able to speak in a whisper, and that an incapability so to do was a sure badge of respectability. Then his curiosity became greater than his pride. 'Are you going to take all the snuff-boxes?' he repeated.

'Only this one,' replied Blackshirt, indicating the box in silver that was in the form of a travelling trunk and which had figures of great beauty in a modified form of bas-relief on the four sides and the lid.

'The most valuable ones are in that far case.'

Blackshirt chuckled. 'I believe you'd like me to take everything—is that how you look after your lord and master's interests?'

The butler's position was simply explained. It was his duty to clean each and every snuff-box once a fortnight—and Mr. Justice Parlant always watched to make certain he forgot none. 'Only wanted to save you trouble,' he grumped. He began to think about the whisky bottle again.

Blackshirt stared at the lock of the door, and there was a strange sense of exasperation within him. Had he not circumscribed his movements by a self-inflicted code of behaviour he could have either taken the key from the sleeping Judge or broken the lock by means of chisel and saw. But he had decided to use nothing other than the pick, and knew that even if it meant failure he would hold fast to that resolution.

'Why are you only taking one?' asked the butler, resolutely turning aside from thoughts of the whisky.

'As a memento of a pleasant evening.'

'Is it true you're a millionaire?'

'Ye gods, no!' Blackshirt replied, surprised.

'That's what my paper said you were, last time it mentioned you.' The butler spoke eagerly. A friend of his had once shaken hands with a man who was the brother of a man who appeared on television: the said friend had never ceased to boast about that moment. Now, the butler would be able to retaliate with great, possibly overwhelming, force.

There was a sudden muffled "click" from the lock, and Blackshirt sighed with relief, swung open the door of the case, took the snuff-box from the shelf on which it had been. Examined closely, it was of even finer workmanship than he had thought.

'The gold one in the other corner cost the Judge two hundred guineas.'

'Did it?' remarked the cracksman.

'It's practically unique.'

Blackshirt stretched across the case and picked up the indicated snuff-box. The butler had been quite right—it was a lovely example of the craft. When he had examined it he replaced it.

'I'll be away soon,' said the cracksman.

'What shall I tell the Judge?'

'Compliment him from me on his good taste.'

The butler shivered. Deliver that message and the Judge would produce a flow of language that, if he heard it in Court from the lips of another, he would castigate the speaker as a foul-mouthed villain.

Blackshirt closed the glass door of the show-case, turned and took the torch from the butler's hands. 'Now comes the question of what to do with you,' he said thoughtfully.

'If I promise not to . . .?' He came to a halt. 'Couldn't you . . .?'

'I'll tie you up loosely and you can gradually work your way free.'

'Could you do it nearer my bedroom?' pleaded the butler. Instinct suddenly told him that if found in the gun-room his wife would show how deeply lay her base suspicions when she accused him of having originally left the bedroom in search of a drink.

'Any particular reason?'

He mumbled something, became red in the face.

Blackshirt chuckled. 'I'll leave you with your own dark secrets. Lead me to wherever it is you want to play the part of a hero.'

The butler rose from the chair on which he had been sitting, hesitated as he tried to overcome the trembling of his legs, and hastily moved forward as the cracksman showed signs of impatience. He opened the door of the gun-room, was about to step out when he was held back by a hand that rested on his right shoulder and gripped him with fierce strength.

They waited, motionless, until Blackshirt was certain all was quiet, then there was a whispered command and they began to walk.

They moved along the heavy carpet that covered half the width of the corridor and passed two doors. They were about to continue past a third door when Blackshirt stopped. Something had attracted his attention. He swung the torch round.

The butler drew in his breath so heavily it was as though he cried out. Then his legs began to tremble more rapidly than ever.

Before them was a thin trickle of blood.

Chapter Two

BLACKSHIRT opened the door of the room, shone his torch inside. He was shocked by what he saw. The Judge had not found death easily.

The butler began to moan, a sound that came from the back of his throat and had about it no more coherence than a child's whimper. The sound became louder.

'Shut up,' snapped Blackshirt.

'He . . . he's been killed.'

'No one'll argue about that.'

'You killed him.'

'I did not.'

'You killed him before I caught you and that's why you wouldn't come in here to get the key of the cabinet.'

'Then why did I come in here a second ago?'

'For God's sake don't kill me.'

Blackshirt shut the door, half dragged, half carried, the butler back into the gun-room.

'You killed him. . . . I tell you, you killed him.'

The butler was so shocked he was scarcely aware of what he was saying or doing. Blackshirt gagged and bound him, left him in the gun-room and returned to where the killing had taken place.

The body of the Judge lay untidily on the floor, head near the door. It was impossible to say from a casual examination which of the many injuries had caused his death. What was certain, however, was that he had been tortured before being finally killed.

Blackshirt examined the room, found nothing of interest. He returned to the butler. 'When you get free, call the police. Tell them exactly what happened, nothing more or less. Is that clear?'

The bound man nodded.

Blackshirt left. He stepped from the gun-room into the passage beyond. The dark closed over the butler and his mind was flooded by the terror of what he knew and what he did not know. He saw a mental picture of the Judge lying on the floor near the door, blood trailing from his head; then there was a shift of focus and it was the butler who lay there so very dead. He thought he heard footsteps approaching, the slight swish as black-sleeved arm rubbed against black shirt on the downward stroke, and for an instant his brain recorded actual pain from the blow. Then some measure of reality returned, but his fears did not lessen, and the sweat sprang from his flesh. He moaned, and the gag turned the sound into a death-rattle.

He heard the clock in the dining-room chime: it had only to be wound once a year, and he recalled what happened the previous year when he had forgotten the annual chore. The memory reminded him that he could not forever lie where he was, supine. He began to struggle, and, as the cracksman had promised, the bonds began to loosen. Encouraged, he rolled backwards and forwards, trying to drag the rope from about his wrists as he did so.

He wrenched one hand free, then the other. He took a handkerchief from his pocket, wiped it across his brow, removed the filthy-tasting gag, untied his feet. He stood up, and there was a sense of the incredulous within him that he should still be alive.

He had been told to call the police. That was to place matters of minor importance in a false position of priority. He set out to rectify such error, entered the pantry, uncovered the bottle of whisky, and drank the greater portion of the contents. The neat spirit acted quickly, and some of the monstrous shadows that had filled his brain retreated. With an emotion that bore some relation to courage, he entered the sitting-room, switched on the electric light, and crossed to the telephone. He began to dial. There was a sound from beyond the door, and not even the whisky could quench the flame of terror that speared through his body.

'What service do you require?' asked a loud voice.

'Police,' he called out, 'and for God's sake hurry, he's come back to kill me.'

'Police,' answered the man, unimpressed by the urgency of the situation.

There was another sound from the door and the butler prepared himself for his last few moments.

'Police here,' said a new voice.

The cause of the sounds identified itself, and he watched the cat enter the room, eyes as evilly cold as ever. He loathed that cat. He would have removed it from the scene a long time ago had it not been the Judge's pride and joy. He remembered that the Judge was dead.

*

Superintendent Ashley climbed out of the car, cigarette hitched to his top lip. He wore a muffler about his neck which, with trousers and coat, hid the pyjamas he still wore, but nothing could obscure the look on his face which was that of a man newly and most unwelcomely brought from his bed.

A constable saluted him as he entered the house. He ignored the politeness. He loathed the world. Five o'clock in the morning was a totally uncivilized hour, especially if one had not reached bed the night before until midnight.

Detective-Sergeant Hooper met him. 'Bad business, sir.'

The Superintendent eyed him with hostility. 'Since when has murder been anything else?' he demanded belligerently.

'This is a particularly nasty one, sir.'

'Go away and tell your horror stories to someone else.' The Superintendent detached the cigarette from his lip as the latter became too hot, dropped it to the ground, trod on it. 'Let's go look see.'

'There's something you ought to know first, sir.'

'Hooper, Fate has been unfair enough to land me with your services, but that doesn't mean I can't try to make the best of a hopeless job. Just lead me to the body, and for the rest, shut up.' He lit another cigarette, attached it to his upper lip.

'In this case, sir——'

'One more word and I'll have you back pounding the beat before breakfast.'

Detective-Sergeant Hooper wondered why it was the Superintendent had never contributed to the statistics of road accidents.

They crossed the hall, mounted the stairs, and continued along the passage until they came to the bedroom. The scene within was one of apparent disorganization, the coherence of which only became apparent to the trained mind.

The Superintendent watched as the photographs were taken. He wondered sadly why murder had to be a nocturnal crime. If one examined the question, there was no reason why it should not occasionally take place during the day, thus allowing the police sometimes to sleep at night.

The doctor crossed to his side. 'Nasty death.'

The Superintendent was about to remark sarcastically that he had not really supposed it to be otherwise, when he checked his words. One was not as rude to a doctor as one was to a sergeant. 'Any particular blow kill him?'

'Can't say until we have a look inside. My guess would be one of those three across the forehead.'

'Are those rope marks on his wrists?'

'They are. Tied down so he could offer no resistance. . . . Someone didn't like him.'

'Think that's so extraordinary?'

'Can't say I'm likely to faint from surprise.'

The Superintendent felt his lips warming up and detached the stub of the cigarette, dropped it to the floor, stamped on it. 'I've given evidence in Court when he's been sitting, and if you'd handed me a twelve bore I'd have blown his head off with the very greatest of pleasure.'

'Never seemed to like policemen, did he?'

'Feeling was mutual.'

'Think this job was done by someone he sent down for a stiff sentence who reckoned it time the account was balanced up?'

'I'd lay a lot of money to that effect,' answered the Superintendent.

The doctor picked up his case. 'I'll be on my way—reckon my bed must be getting lonely.' He left the room. The sheeted body of the Judge was carried away on a stretcher, the photographers left, the room emptied of people until there were only two men left.

Detective-Sergeant Hooper coughed.

'Where's everybody?' asked the Superintendent.

'Gathered in the main sitting-room, sir.'

'Gathered? What's up, going harvesting?'

'Sir. . . . About this case.'

'Something tells me you're about to try and solve it. Remember what happened last time you did that?'

'I had a word with the butler and he said——'

The Superintendent spoke with furious sarcasm. 'He heard a suspicious sound at one twenty-two exactly, and as he came downstairs to investigate he came face to face with the murderer.'

'How did you guess, sir?' asked the other, insolently refusing to show any signs of triumph.

'What the devil do you mean?'

'Blackshirt, sir.'

There was a long silence. The Superintendent took a packet of cigarettes from his pocket and offered it to the other. Such act showed the measure of his astonishment.

*

'All in black,' said the butler.

'Of course he was all in black,' snapped the Superintendent.

'It's creepy to see him.'

'Keep off the whisky and maybe you won't get the horrors so often.'
There was no mistaking the rich aroma that accompanied the butler.

'If you'd gone through what I've gone through——'

'I'll put your name in for the V.C.' The Superintendent was far too tired
to offer any verbal courtesies. 'What gloves was he wearing? What kind of
hood or mask?'

The questions were numerous, and by the time the butler was allowed to
leave the room he had the feeling he was suspected of a dozen crimes and
could expect to be arrested before sundown.

'I just don't get it, Bill,' said Superintendent Ashley, as the door closed
and left the two policemen alone.

Hooper relaxed. The use of his Christian name indicated that,
temporarily, his senior was going to display a few of the attributes of the
human race. 'You mean it being Blackshirt?'

'Yes. Find the Crown Jewels pinched, and he's your man, laughing like
hell to himself. But this—this isn't his line of country.'

'I've never gone all the way with thinking of him as someone who'll
always play the game according to his own queer code.'

'He's done so for a hell of a long time.'

'That means nothing.'

'Doesn't it?' The Superintendent stood up and began to pace the floor.
'Piece together all you've ever heard about this fellow and you'll get a
picture of a man who's having fun. That's not the chap who'll kill in the
most vicious of ways.'

'It'll take more than that to ignore the fact he was here after the snuff-
boxes.'

'One snuff-box.'

'Maybe he'd marked the Judge down a long time ago, or perhaps the
opportunity, when presented, was too attractive.'

'I'm not convinced.'

Hooper yawned, stretched his arms above his head. 'If it wasn't
Blackshirt, it means two people broke into here during the night. Isn't that
asking a bit much?'

'Nothing more than a simple coincidence, and when you've been at the job as long as I have you won't sneer at such a possibility quite so readily. Can you deny without fear of contradiction that the whole of life is one huge coincidence? Two people meet because they want to catch the same bus at the same time on the same day, and . . .'

Hooper tried not to listen, but that was a difficult task. He had heard the speech so often, he knew it as well as the speaker, which meant that the words, unbidden, formed in his mind. He wondered why the Superintendent was so stupid in many ways. True, Blackshirt had not killed before, but why should that fact have the slightest relevance to the question of whether he had killed in this case? Besides, perhaps he considered his act was justified. Many people would have agreed that the Judge's death was an overdue sign of the maturity of the state of civilization.

*

Ashley stared at the three men who had been the Judge's guests, and decided none of them showed any signs of reasonable humanity, and especially was this so with regard to the bearded Panton, the painter, a name he thought he ought to recognize but was uncertain whether he did. Ashley's knowledge of art began and ceased with the Mona Lisa, and in his slightly puritanical mind all painters lived in a bohemian state that taxed even the powers of the Sunday newspapers to describe in publishable form.

'Are we going to be allowed to return to our rooms before the dinner gong is sounded?' asked Montgomery officiously.

Funny people, retired army colonels, thought the Superintendent sourly. Never learn that their newly-found fellow civilians aren't rosy-cheeked subalterns. It was only colonels who failed to appreciate the transition; other ranks became almost normal, given time. 'Shan't keep you a moment longer than I have to, sir,' he replied. He waited for further comment, was surprised when it did not come. 'If I could speak to each of you in turn in the next room?'

They made no answer.

The Superintendent left the room, sat down behind the desk in the library and waited for Hooper to join him. When the latter entered he spoke even before he had closed the door. 'They've found the drain-pipe he used and the window he forced, and there's one fairly good shoe-imprint in a flower-bed.'

17

'Strange.' Ashley stared at the far wall. 'You don't expect Blackshirt to leave footmarks.'

'He's not infallible.'

'When you've been in the force as long as I have, you won't tempt fate by saying such a thing.' He loosened his muffler because his neck was too warm, hoped the top of his pyjamas did not show. The Colonel would consider that the very depths of depravity. 'Yule, tell the first one to come in.' The constable who had been standing by the door turned and left the room. The Superintendent thought how stupid some people's names were.

Edward Fisher sat down in the chair to which he was directed and tried to intimate he was completely at ease, with the result that he gave the impression of complete guilt. He was extremely worried because his wife was away, taking a cure, and when she heard with what he had got himself entangled she would become most annoyed. He tried to tell the policemen that, but found they were not interested in his troubles. He sighed. Life could be very harsh, especially to a man who had to pay as much super-tax as did he.

Colonel Montgomery was the second man to be interviewed, and, much to his surprise, found himself answering the questions put to him. This annoyed him and he began to mention India, but the infamous police ignored his words and continued to treat him as though he might be the murderer. The Colonel became more angry.

Richard Panton said quite freely that his success as a painter was not exactly overwhelming, and the Superintendent was greatly relieved. It was annoying not to know whether one were talking to fame. Made it so difficult to decide whether the speaker's words were clever or not.

The butler was then called in, and he indignantly pointed out that as a victim of a barbarity nearly as great as that which had killed the Judge, he should be treated kindly, not subjected to continuous questioning, apparently designed to prove him a second Jack the Ripper. The Superintendent said he probably was, and laughed, which showed the extent of his ill-breeding.

Other people were interrogated, but their evidence was purely negative.

The Superintendent sighed as the door closed on the last person, and undid the muffler so that his neck was free. He ran a hand over his forehead. He had never been a man who could become tired gracefully: lack of sleep produced within his skull physical pain.

'The three guests are a case of the wise monkeys,' remarked Hooper.

'What the devil are you talking about?'

'See nothing, hear nothing, speak nothing.'

'Don't talk rubbish.'

'Sorry.'

There was a knock at the door and a man entered. 'Let's have the full story,' he said cheerfully.

The Superintendent spoke angrily. 'How in the name of hell did you sniff this one out?'

'Got a nose that can smell a murder fifty miles away.' The speaker was a reporter who boasted that no serious crime had ever escaped him. Senior officials of Scotland Yard would have given much to know his sources of information. 'What about pictures?'

Ashley hastily did up his muffler, hiding from sight his brightly coloured pyjamas. 'No photos.'

'Let's have the story then.'

'Parlant had his head knocked in.'

'Three cheers for that.'

'You ought to have more respect for the dead,' snapped the Superintendent.

'Wouldn't put it past you to have done the dirty deed. Remember the pasting he gave you in Court during the Rush case?'

Ashley decided that if ever he were in a position of power he would shut down all newspapers and jail all reporters, thus ensuring the freedom of the subject.

The reporter managed to learn a little of what had happened, but could uncover nothing that would startle the readers of his newspaper. He therefore ignored the express order to leave the house by the shortest route, and by devious means, of which he was a master, made verbal contact with the butler.

'Interesting case, isn't it?' he said.

'I would never refer to the death of my late master in such terms,' answered the butler haughtily, happy to meet someone to whom he could be rude.

'You're the exception that proves the rule. Know anything of interest?'

'Nothing.'

'It was you that found the body, wasn't it?'

'I was forced so to do, yes.'

The reporter did not speak until he could conceal the excitement those words caused. 'That's a funny way of putting it,' he finally remarked with enforced casualness. He fingered the five pound note he always carried. Nothing was such a stimulant to the vocal chords as was that.

'Funny!' The butler was disgusted. 'I'm glad someone can find humour at the thought of the position in which I was. About to be murdered in cold blood.'

'Murdered—you?' The reporter sounded disbelieving.

The butler was indignant that any doubt should be shown to his words. 'You try having Blackshirt immediately behind you threatening to skewer you to the floor-boards with a knife three feet long and see if you don't think you might be murdered.'

'Blackshirt? You saw him?'

'I keep telling you, he stood behind me and threatened me, then made me hold the torch for him.'

'What's he look like?'

'Black.'

'Tell me what happened, starting at the beginning.'

'I have informed the police of all that occurred, and am certainly not going to repeat myself,' announced the butler grandly. He left.

The reporter transferred the five pound note from one pocket to another—thereby symbolizing an entry in his expense sheet. He turned and hurriedly made his way out of the house. He had found the headlines.

Chapter Three

VERRELL studied the newspaper with angry distaste. He looked up at Roberts, his valet. 'Thanks for nothing.'

'I thought you would wish to see it, sir.'

'I'd rather not have done so,' he replied. The tone of his voice indicated clearly what he would have liked to have done to the author of the article in which it was made all too clear that the police considered Blackshirt to have been the murderer of the Judge.

'It looks as though the only evidence is what the butler said, sir.'

Verrell muttered something. He felt it mattered not how suspect was the information—the result was the same. Anger built up within him. Blackshirt had always been the cracksman who stole for the fun of it, who made of his battle with the police a game. Blackshirt the murderer formed the antithesis of such picture.

'What happened, sir?' asked Roberts, who took a personal pride in Blackshirt's exploits.

The story was soon told.

'Bad luck, choosing that one night.'

'You can say that again, and underline it six times.' Verrell stood up, crossed to the window and stared below. 'Even so, half the trouble has been caused by the garrulous old fool of a butler. I reckon someone should have a word with him.'

Roberts coughed. 'Have you any idea, sir?'

'Idea about what?'

'What actually happened?'

'The old boy was deader than a leg of mutton when I saw him.'

'The report says he had a pretty nasty death.'

'Wasn't pretty.'

Roberts left the room. It was a moment when Verrell needed solitude that he might plan the future. Roberts felt sorry for the butler.

*

The butler smiled in his sleep. He was dreaming about his bank balance which was in a remarkably healthy state considering the strictness with which Mr. Justice Parlant had always investigated accounts. But then, the butler had had a long training.

With the suddenness that so often characterized dreams, the scene changed from momentary bliss to watery agony. It seemed to the butler as though the four elements had been reduced to one.

He gradually became certain he was awake, and the knowledge was painful. It was distressing to dream of being inundated: to find such mental image was no more than reality was infinitely worse. Searching for cause, he decided the notoriously bad plumbing must be at fault.

A further, and unwanted, thought occurred to him. He knew, for certain fact, there were no water-pipes above his room.

He opened his eyes. By the side of his bed, empty water-jug in one hand, stood a figure clothed in black.

'My apologies,' said Blackshirt. He pointed to the second bed. 'And to your wife, who fainted when she saw me.'

The butler wished the other were not always so infernally polite. It seemed to make everything so much more deadly. At the thought of that last word he groaned. He remembered how the Judge had looked, and all too easily imagined his own body in similar disrepair.

The cracksman spoke. 'You'll not be surprised to hear I read the newspaper today.'

At the time the butler had thought the article was one in the eye for Blackshirt; now he was not so certain. 'I didn't say anything,' he hurriedly muttered.

'You gave an exclusive interview.'

'I didn't know the man was a reporter.'

'Does that make any difference to the fact that you stated I threatened to smash in your skull as I had done the Judge's?'

'I didn't say anything of the sort.'

'Then from whence the report?'

'How should I know? I swear I told him nothing.'

'What did you actually say?'

'Only that . . . that you'd . . . .'

'Whatever you thought up in your imagination as my having said won't be a patch on what my instincts tell me to do now.'

The butler decided dignity was an over-expensive luxury, and began to plead for mercy, enumerating the wonderful qualities of the real Blackshirt, a man so filled with the love of his fellow creatures he would not hurt a fly.

The cracksman stared at the butler and regretfully decided the sudden soaking and ensuing fright was as much punishment as he could inflict. 'Staying here?' he asked abruptly.

'Not in this house. It wouldn't be seemly—not after the Judge is buried.'

'Just remaining long enough to make certain of first pickings?'

'Certainly not,' denied the butler indignantly, horrified that anyone could have so easily divined his intentions.

'What's happened to the three guests?'

'Gone back to their homes.'

'Was no one else in this house last night?'

'Only the other staff.'

Blackshirt left the room without speaking. The butler, uncertain whether the intruder had gone permanently, lay motionless, lacking the courage to move. Time passed. Something crawled slowly over his sparse hair, settled midway between his ears, and began to dig in. The need to scratch was great, increased because he forced his hands to remain at his sides. By now, it seemed as though the intruder were busy burrowing deep within his flesh, and into his mind came stories he had heard of insects that bored through the flesh until they reached the brain, whereupon they were happy, but the owner was not. The fright occasioned by this pathetic picture overcame his fear of the absent Blackshirt, and he hastily scratched most vigorously. The insect ceased to burrow, and since his movements had provoked no sudden return of the cracksman, he sat up in bed, then, with a feeling of pride in his own courage, reached over to the telephone. He dialled three nines, informed the police of all that had happened. Instead of immediate promises of armoured cars there was a long pause, then finally he was connected with the Superintendent who had visited the house when the police investigations had been in progress.

'What's happened?' said the weary voice.

The butler noticed his wife was conscious, ignored her pleas for help, answered the Superintendent in great detail with many references to the dangers he had had to undergo because of the lack of police protection.

'You're not harmed?'

'No, but——'

'Maybe you'll have learned, then, to keep quiet when some paper-snooper asks you questions.' The connection went dead.

The butler stared at the receiver. He swore he would write to his member of Parliament, then remembered he had no idea who that was. He felt much aggrieved.

*

Edward Fisher snored in his sleep. The sound began low down in the scale, rose rapidly, ended on a note that was half whistle, half grunt. The noise partially explained why his wife took the cure so frequently.

Fisher awoke suddenly, looked up, and there was Blackshirt.

'Know anything about the murder?' asked the cracksman.

His mind somersaulted into panic. 'What——'

'Who killed Parlant?'

'I don't know anything.'

'Certain?'

'I told the police I didn't.'

'I'm not the police.' Blackshirt's voice became cold and angry. 'I'm working alone, and I'm not binding myself by any rules of conduct.'

'What do you want? If it's my wife's jewels, they're all at the bank.'

'Who killed Parlant?'

'I didn't know anything about it until they woke me and told me.'

'You heard nothing that night?'

'Nothing—I sleep very soundly. We had a late meal, sat over the port for a long while, then went to bed. That's all I can tell you.'

'I hope you're not lying.'

Fisher shivered. He knew he was not lying, but did Blackshirt? And at the thought of what would happen to him if the cracksman refused to believe the truth, he shivered some more.

*

Montgomery, Colonel, treated a similar intrusion in a very different manner. On being awakened he reached into the top drawer of the small bed-side table, jerked out his revolver—signed for in the army records as having been lost—and pulled the trigger several times in quick succession. Great was his consternation and anger when nothing happened. He pulled the trigger several more times, watched by a motionless Blackshirt.

The Colonel broke open the revolver to the accompaniment of a soldierly oath and stared at the empty chambers, knowing full well that when he had gone to bed he had checked, as always, that the gun was loaded and that the hammer rested on an empty chamber.

Blackshirt opened one hand and showed the five cartridges he held. He advanced, sat down on the edge of the bed.

The Colonel, undecided between the desire never to surrender and to remain uninjured, hesitated. The delay decided him and for perhaps the first time in his career, which happily had never called for the use of such faculty, he listened to common sense and did nothing.

Blackshirt interrogated him, calmly, quietly, and with the ease and aplomb of one who was doing something quite ordinary. Much to his subsequent disgust, the Colonel answered in like manner, and it was not until he was alone once more, with the cartridges thrown on the foot of the bed, that he recovered. He reloaded. 'Come back here and I'll fill you so full of lead you'll rattle like an Ashanti war dance,' he snapped, addressing, with great bravery, the empty air.

*

As he had done the previous twice, Blackshirt searched the flat before he awoke the occupier. There was little of interest in Panton's studio-flat, except for the paintings. These he studied at some length, eventually deciding that first impressions were correct. He did not like them.

He awoke Panton, asked him the same questions he had Fisher and Montgomery, learned nothing. The murderer had entered and left the house in complete silence—and since entry had been made by way of a drainpipe and locked window which had to be forced, there was further evidence of much skill.

'Now what?' asked Panton interestedly, when it was clear the cracksman had temporarily nothing more to say.

'Future plans are undecided.'

'You must be very touchy of your reputation to go to all this trouble merely to try and show you didn't bump off the old boy.'

'It's a form of insurance should I ever suffer the misfortune of being caught—I don't relish being tried for murder.'

'Strikes me you're really far more concerned with your reputation.'

Blackshirt remained silent. What the other said was perfectly true.

'You do maintain you didn't do it, don't you?'

'Yes.'

'I don't know whether to believe you, or not.'

'I'm not suggesting you should do either,' snapped the cracksman.

'On the contrary, by asking such questions as you have done, consciously or sub-consciously, you're trying to convince me of your innocence. That being so, I can only repeat, I'm not decided.' He held up one hand in a pacific gesture. 'Don't get too annoyed. You should be grateful that I can visualize you as innocent—after what's been written in the papers, I imagine I'm in the minority when I do that.'

Blackshirt left. He had learned but one thing. Nothing would ever make him understand, far less like, a painting by Richard Panton.

*

Superintendent Ashley lowered the telephone receiver on to its cradle. He picked up the mug of coffee, drank from it. 'Bill,' he groaned, 'go out and shoot Blackshirt for me, will you—as a personal favour?'

'Not another one?'

He nodded. 'Another one. Mr. Richard Panton wishes to report he had just been visited by Blackshirt who asked him numerous questions. . . . What the devil do all these people expect us to do? Go and soothe their fevered brows just because Blackshirt—who seems incapable of sleeping at night-time, as opposed to myself who isn't given the chance—drops in on them? They ought to consider themselves blasted lucky he didn't take half their homes with him.'

'What do you reckon is going on?' asked Hooper, every bit as tired as his superior, but not allowed to make a song and dance about it.

'If you can't work that one out it's time you applied for your pension.' The Superintendent lit a cigarette, and, for once, smoked it in a normal manner. 'As I said from the very beginning, Blackshirt didn't kill the old basket. It's not his hall-mark. Someone did it, and Blackshirt was unlucky enough to be visiting the same place at the same time.'

'I can't go along with you there.'

'Who the devil asked you to?'

'I was only saying——'

'I know precisely what you were saying, Bill, but don't bother. Just take my word for it, Blackshirt didn't commit this murder, and we've got a hell of a long row before us if we're to find out who did.'

'You're the boss.'

'That's right.' The Superintendent drained the mug. 'Any more coffee knocking about?'

'Might be able to squeeze another half-cup.'

'See what you can do—if I don't drink something, I'll fall asleep before you can say Jack Robinson.'

Detective-Sergeant Hooper stood up, collected the other's cup, slowly made his way along the brightly lit corridor until he came to the small cupboard-like space in which was a gas-ring and a tap. He checked that there was still some liquid left in the pot, placed it on the ring and lit the gas. He wondered why Ashley was so stubborn in his refusal to believe the truth. Blackshirt had committed the murder. All the circumstantial evidence pointed to that fact, and as was well known, witnesses might lie, but circumstances could not. Only two questions remained to be answered. What was the motive, and why had so vicious a means of death been chosen? Hooper leaned back against the wall. Why should the cracksman have chosen such a way in which to kill? Why should he have killed? Had he some old score against the Judge? . . . Yet state that he had done the killing, and the questions became, for the moment, superfluous. Hooper suddenly sighed deeply. Of course, the knowledge that the murderer was Blackshirt would bring no cheer to anyone. The police had been trying for so long to catch the cracksman, there could be none now who would rate their chances of success at anything but the longest odds.

The coffee boiled noisily and Hooper went to lift the pot from the gas-ring, burned his hand on the handle. He swore. He did that practically every time he made, or reheated, coffee.

'Been growing the coffee beans?' asked Ashley sarcastically when the other returned to the room.

'Been thinking.'

'I'll thank you to do one thing at a time in future—let's have coffee and forget the whole affair. Who the hell cares if old Parlant was killed? Best thing that's happened this year.'

They drank their coffee. They were working long after they need have done, so much so, that there was nothing they could immediately do but sit and think. Yet that was what Ashley liked to do. He mentally assembled all the facts, then thought about them. Sometimes it was amazing what progress he made by such means.

*

Verrell had returned from Panton's flat annoyed because he had learned nothing, annoyed that such fact should annoy him, since it was precisely as he had expected. His mind churned over the facts until he was in bed, then he managed to banish all thoughts of the murder. He slept until an hour so late it automatically marked him as either vagabond or author.

He ate breakfast and studied the newspapers Roberts had placed by the side of his plate. Not one of them made any report on the further visits of Blackshirt the previous night, but confined themselves to still more discussions of the murder, taking full advantage of the news value to be obtained from the violent death of a judge and the presence of the notorious cracksman.

'Some more coffee, sir?'

'Thanks.'

Roberts poured out the coffee, added the precise amount of milk. 'Any luck, sir?'

'Not so much as the smell of one.' Verrell lit a cigarette. 'The only progress I've made has been backwards, and as from now I can't see that there's anything I can do to reverse the process.'

'Reading between the lines, sir, it doesn't look as if the police are making any headway, either.'

'When they're certain I'm the guilty one, they don't have to, do they?'

Roberts folded his arms. 'Do you think they're quite so certain?'

'Who can resist a coincidence that solves everything?' Verrell finished his coffee, flicked the ash from the end of his cigarette. He stared out of the window. Roberts cleared the table, left the room.

Where could he, Verrell, begin? To clear the name of Blackshirt he had to find the murderer, but where was he to start looking? He had, already, let it be known—in such places as the announcement would take effect— that there was a rich reward for information, but murderers were single workers who did not boast about their exploits. He did not expect to learn anything from that direction. Then where was he to turn? Search the house of the Judge? He had done so, found nothing. Interrogate the participants once more? The same applied. That left what? He grinned wryly. What indeed?

He cheered up slightly. He held one great advantage over the police. They believed Blackshirt to be the murderer: he knew that was not so.

Someone had tortured, then killed, the Judge. Was this the act of a man seeking revenge? It might be, but it seemed a hell of a way of going about it. Would not the Judge's death have sufficed? The added torture seemed to speak of a personal hatred beyond any that was fostered by the administration of the law.

Was it information that had been sought? What information could a Judge hold that a killer would need or want?

Verrell stood up, crossed to the next room, sat down in an armchair. Facing him was a clock that showed he should have started writing twenty-four minutes before. Having overshot that time there seemed no point in not overshooting it some more. His publishers had always previously been kind about delivery dates.

Who and Why? Learn the why, and possibly the who would answer itself.

He lit a second cigarette, decided that life was pretty damn' complicated. He grinned. That was the way he liked it.

Eventually he managed to settle down to his writing, and by the use of a great deal of mental will-power forgot the questions that seemed to be without answers.

That night, when it was dark, he moved restlessly about the flat. There must be something he could do, yet he could not name it. The need for action became too great, and he dressed in Blackshirt clothes, tied white scarf about his neck, and left the flat. Without conscious volition he found his way to the Judge's house, and accepting this as an omen, despite the facts, stepped into the shadow of a tree and removed white scarf, donned black hood and gloves.

He searched the house yet again, found nothing. The place was empty, even the butler having left. He checked on the drain-pipe the intruder had climbed the night of the murder and noted that it was a difficult climb.

He left the house, removed hood and gloves, replaced the scarf, resumed his walk. Far from easing his mind, the visit had made him more restless, and he knew there was only one thing to be done. As a distant clock struck the hour he stopped, checked on the house he was opposite, and then broke into it. It seemed only typical that the building should be filled with furniture of incredibly bad taste and should contain a safe that was empty.

Chapter Four

Two of the newspapers on Verrell's breakfast table next morning headlined the news. A third referred to the event in small print in a paragraph relegated to one of the pages that were read only by the vulgarly curious.

The various reports were unusually consistent. Blackshirt had broken into the home of Harold Brindle, a solicitor, had threatened to murder Brindle at the first sign of opposition, searched the house for something that was never specified, then left, after another threat against the solicitor's life.

Verrell read the description of the cracksman, noted he had worn black hood, shirt and gloves in addition to a black suit. Verrell wanted to swear to relieve some of the anger that was within him, but knew such words would not have the required effect and therefore contained them. Roberts came into the room.

'Read them?' asked Verrell.

'Yes, sir.'

'Someone's pinching my copyright.'

'It wasn't you then?'

He spoke sharply. 'Since when have I acted in that way?'

'I thought maybe you'd visited the solicitor and he'd made up the rest of the story.'

'Why the hell should he do a thing like that? He's probably a most respectable member of his profession.'

'Is there such a combination, sir?'

Verrell smiled briefly. 'You've a point there.' His expression became grim once more. 'By the time I've finished with him he'll learn what a commissioner of oaths really means.'

'Perhaps he thought you were the real Blackshirt?'

'Why the devil didn't he take the trouble to check?' retorted Verrell, with all the passion of illogical indignation.

Roberts remained silent and impassive, a remarkable feat since his mind was visualizing a succession of householders enquiring of the intruding cracksman whether he were the genuine article or not, and refusing to be satisfied until he assured them he was.

'Is there any more coffee?' asked Verrell suddenly.

'Yes, sir.'

Roberts poured out the coffee, then retired from the breakfast-room. Once outside, he allowed his features to relax and he smiled. There was a trace of sympathy in his expression. He was thinking of the poor solicitor.

*

Blackshirt studied the house and reflected that Mr. Harold Brindle must find the pickings of the law even more lucrative than did most. At a time when size was a deterrent, it was strange to see a very large Victorian house occupied by only the one person. Similar buildings on either side had in every case been turned into flats.

He waited under the cover of a tree, tattered and past its prime as were others nearby, and watched the light in the first floor room. Brindle kept late nights.

Twenty minutes after he had taken up position the light was switched off, and then the only illumination about him came from a street lamp twenty yards along the road. This gave sufficient light to pick out substance from nothing, but was not strong enough to produce definite shadows.

Blackshirt remained motionless, alert, but allowed his mind to roam where it wished. He thought about the weather they had suffered recently and wondered if his conscience would agree that it was time he had a holiday, even though he had not long returned from one—a writer needed frequent changes of scene if he were to keep his mind flexible. He heard the measured tread of a patrolling constable and waited for any audible variation in pace. The man came abreast of where he stood, continued on his way. The sound of footsteps became fainter, finally all was silent. Blackshirt wondered whether the south of France or Spain was to be preferred, had his meditations interrupted by the deep rumble of some vintage car thundering its way home with a noise beloved by the owner but not by most others.

It was time to move. He stepped from under the cover of the tree and crossed the ill-kept lawn to reach the concrete path that ran down the side of the house.

He came to the door and checked, opened it within thirty seconds. He made certain there was no form of burglar-alarm, closed the door behind him, took the torch from his belt of tools, and adjusting the shutter so that only a pin-prick of light showed, examined the space in which he was.

Blackshirt carefully made his way up to the bedroom, and reached it without there having been a sound to betray his presence. It was amazing that any man could move so noiselessly.

He entered the bedroom, examined the sleeper by torchlight, then sat down on the side of the bed, shook the other by the shoulders.

Brindle awoke suddenly, opened his eyes, saw the black hand on his shoulder, and cried out from fright.

'No noise,' said a voice that was icy calm.

'Who . . .?'

'Do you need three guesses?'

'What . . .?'

Blackshirt moved the torch until it shone on his hood.

'Blackshirt!' Brindle's voice was shrill.

'Correct in one.'

'Why have you come back?'

'Back?'

Brindle gave no answer.

'Why did you give that story to the newspapers?'

'They came and interviewed me.'

'It was a pack of lies.'

'It . . . it wasn't. That's what happened.'

'I was nowhere near here last night.'

Brindle licked his lips with a tongue that refused to wet them. 'You came and . . .'

'It was not I.'

'You—the man who was here was dressed in black exactly like you. He said he was Blackshirt.'

'He spoke those words?'

'Yes.'

Blackshirt wondered what his future conduct must be, finally spoke. 'Tell me what happened, and assure yourself that if you make one mistake you'll never mulct another customer.'

Brindle was a large man, and when he shifted the bed complained with a low-pitched squeak. His face was almost round and so fat the flesh about his eyes made them look much smaller than they really were.

Brindle related what had happened, speaking nervously, but coherently. He had been sleeping, had been awakened by the figure in black who demanded the keys to the safe, threatened to smash in his head if he made a sound. The intruder had bound and gagged him, left the room, returned later and demanded to know the whereabouts of other hiding-places. On being informed there were none, there had been a succession of threats, but no violent action. Finally satisfied the repeated denials were the truth, the man had left.

'Did he wear the same kind of hood as I am wearing?' asked Blackshirt, once the other had finished speaking.

'Near enough.'

'What was his speaking voice like?'

'Why all these questions?'

'How did he speak?' snapped the cracksman.

Brindle accepted the fact that objections on his part were to be eschewed. 'Very much as you do.'

'How very much?'

'I shouldn't like to be required to tell one from the other.'

'What was stolen?'

'Nothing.'

'Are you certain of that?'

'Perfectly—there's nothing in this house worth taking.'

Blackshirt was puzzled by Brindle. The solicitor spoke as though convinced the intruder of the present night was the same as that of the previous one, and only answered the questions to humour the cracksman, yet . . . 'What was this other man after?'

'I don't know.'

'You must have some idea.'

'Are you telling me—or asking me?'

Blackshirt leaned forward and his voice hardened. 'Get this straight, Brindle, somebody has thrown down the gauntlet by wearing the dress that is exclusively mine. I aim to accept the gage and discover his identity. Anyone who hinders me is liable to get hurt.'

Brindle, who had been telling himself he was not afraid, rapidly decided he had been guilty of mendacity. No specific threats had been made, which left his all-too-active mind free to imagine. He was surprised by the extent of that imagination. He spoke, and the words slurred one into another because of the speed with which he did so. 'He never said what he wanted to find.'

'Papers? Jewellery? Money?'

'I seldom bring papers back here, and there's no jewellery and only a handful of money in the house.'

'Then why have a safe?'

'If I do bring back work, I always keep the papers locked in the safe when I'm not actually studying them.'

Blackshirt tried to add up the score, found he got so many different answers it was useless. He stood up, paced the room twice. He was worried. Instinct warned him that something was very wrong, yet he could not name what.

He decided he could do no more than search the house and hope such search would afford him more of a lead than the prospects would suggest. The circumstances being what they were, he saw no reason why he should not take advantage of all possible short cuts. 'Where are the keys of the safe?'

'I haven't got them—the police took them away.'

'Why?'

'They said they wanted to examine them.'

'What did they hope to find?'

Brindle shook his head. 'I don't know.'

'You're remarkably ill-informed.'

Why should the police take the keys? Did the fact that they had, suggest anything?

'Turn over,' said Blackshirt abruptly.

'Why?'

'There's no place for argument.'

Brindle did as had been ordered. He lay, face pressing into the pillow, a quivering mound of fear. His hands and arms were bound, then he was rolled over and a gag inserted into his mouth.

Blackshirt stared at the bound figure. The solicitor had acted as would a stupid man, yet if one thing were certain, it was that he was no fool. What lay behind this apparent contradiction?

The cracksman left the bedroom, examined the rest of the house. The rooms were large and disproportionate, yet sufficient taste had been exercised in choice of furniture and hangings to lend to them a certain elegance.

He discovered the safe in the fourth room he entered. It was old, solid, and ugly. It stood at the far end of the floor, unadorned.

He knew the make of safe, could judge that it would take between half and three-quarters of an hour to open. He undipped the belt of tools from about his waist, laid it on top of the safe, took from it a set of blank keys.

His estimate of time proved to be correct. Thirty-eight minutes after beginning, he forced back the tumblers of the lock, opened the safe door.

Had he accepted Brindle's word, he would have saved himself much trouble. The safe was empty of everything but dust, and of that there was great quantity.

He checked that the safe did not have a false back or side, found nothing. He grinned wryly. Nothing was a word that appeared more and more frequently.

The sound of a car being driven at great speed which braked to a screeching halt outside the house he was in reminded him that frequently nothing was preferable to something. By the time he had crossed to the window the four policemen were already out of the car, sprinting towards the house. He heard the noisy approach of a second car, then a third.

Brindle must have broken loose and given the alarm. Yet how? Blackshirt did not reckon to tie knots that came undone.

The police would not enter the house immediately. By checking on the present whereabouts of Brindle, Blackshirt might lose thirty seconds of escape time, but would gain satisfaction of mind. He moved rapidly.

He opened the door of Brindle's bedroom, stepped inside, directed his torch towards the bed. Sound as were his nerves, what he saw shocked him into immobility for an appreciable length of time. Brindle had given no alarm. He was dead, with head most terribly battered.

Blackshirt checked on the room. Nothing had changed—except Brindle.

He knew now that his instinct, developed until it formed a sixth sense, had been trying to warn him that there had been someone else in the house—the man who had waited to close the trap.

He looked out of the window. The ground was all but invisible, due to the number of policemen who were there. As he watched, a group of four, led by a man who carried an enormous torch, ran along the side of the building and then out of sight. They would be covering the back.

Blackshirt supposed that if mice could think, their thoughts at the moment of capture would be very similar to his present ones. Lured by a piece of cheese, voracious appetite brought disaster. Lured by the report of one who had masqueraded as himself, angry indignation had directed Blackshirt into the trap. The snap of the jaws closing was a filthy and vicious sound.

He tried to think of some way in which he could work to escape the inevitable. Beneath his hood, his face was grim. Given a sporting chance, he enjoyed doing battle. No better than the next man did he welcome abject and unconditional surrender.

He left the room in which he was, checked from others on the same floor as to the positions in which the police had placed themselves. What he saw confirmed what he had expected. The house was encircled.

Was there the slightest chance that he might escape? Observation, logic and experience said no. Those three rarely lied.

*

The senior of the sergeants had set the cordon of men about the building. Satisfied that this task had been carried out as exactly as was possible, he then waited, content that someone would be coming to take responsibility from his shoulders.

Knight arrived, stared at the building, and wished himself many miles away. Some of his colleagues had tried to corner Blackshirt in the past; inevitably they had ended up on the debit side of events. He, Knight, had always been ready to laugh at such stories, since other people's misfortunes naturally were conducive to scornful mockery. He began to realize there might well be two sides to the question.

'All exits covered,' reported the Sergeant.

'Seen anything?'

'Nothing, sir.'

'Call may have been a hoax.'

'Yes, sir.'

'How many doors are there?'

'One in front, one at the back.'

'Windows?'

'Several on each wall. They're all covered, sir.'

'What you mean is, you hope they are.'

And so do you, muttered the Sergeant to himself.

They were silent, and could hear the sounds caused by the men who surrounded the house. Someone had a short but fierce bout of coughing, another cleared his throat, a third shifted his weight from one foot to another and the gravel gave out a sharp crunching noise.

'Have you tried to rouse anyone inside?' asked Knight.

'Not yet, sir.'

'I reckon we should have awakened them by now if there were anyone—but anyway, have a try before we go in.'

A constable pulled the very ornate bell handle, struck the brass knocker, sounded the bell once more. There was no response from within.

'We'll force our way in,' said Knight. He looked round, detailed eight men to follow him, ordered the rest to double their watchfulness.

He went up to the door and turned the handle, and much to his surprise the door opened. He entered the house, followed immediately by the others.

Their torches lit up the hall and all was quiet and peaceful. A constable stepped across to a light switch and pressed the catch down; nothing happened.

'Blast,' said Knight. 'We'll have to take things twice as slowly.'

As he finished speaking there was a pause during which no one moved. In this period they heard, clearly and loudly, a thud from one of the upstairs rooms, then the noise of smashing glass.

'He's up there!' shouted Knight. It sounded as though a struggle had been going on, and as he raced forward and up the stairs, followed by his men, a strange thought formed in his mind. There was no way in which Blackshirt could break loose, therefore the impossible had happened and the cracksman had finally been brought to bay.

They reached the landing above, hesitated. All was quiet. Knight aimed his torch to the right, the direction in which he thought the sounds had come. 'Try that room first,' he ordered.

Three constables moved quickly to the command. The leading one flung back the door, rushed inside, sweeping his torch from side to side; his companions closely backed him up. The room was apparently empty of persons. After they had searched such hiding places as there were, it became certain it was so. They returned to the landing.

Three other men had checked the room to the left, and they reappeared at the same moment.

'Check the next two rooms,' ordered Knight.

They found the body of Brindle.

Knight ran into the room as his name was called out. 'Good God!' he said. He had been prepared to find many things; not this.

37

They all heard the cry that came from below. It began as a call for help, was choked into silence.

*

Because the old trick had become so hackneyed no one would have dared use it; even on the stage it was considered obsolete. Which was a very good reason for relying on it . . . provided one did not blanch at the thought of the odds against it succeeding.

Blackshirt had summed up the situation all too easily. The police had surrounded the house and were in sufficient force to search it and cover the outside at the same time. Therefore, no normal means of escape would be effective. That being so, only abnormal means remained, and it was at this moment of truth that he had considered the front door. Even as he accepted that space as being the only one in which he might successfully find concealment, he shuddered to think what would be said should he be found there. He would become the target for all the psychiatrists in the country.

He tied one end of a length of twine to a small oriental stool, and on top of the latter placed a silver tray and several glasses. He unwound the twine as he made his way downstairs, then stood behind the front door which he unlocked. The feeling of vulnerability within him was as great as if he had been standing in Piccadilly Circus in the rush hour in his Blackshirt clothes.

The bell was rung, the knocker of the door was struck, the bell rang again. He wondered if he had ever taken such a chance before.

The door was opened, and because it did not come right back, Blackshirt pulled it until it did. He needed the maximum cover that could be obtained—if the word "cover" could be used in such circumstances.

He waited, heard the light-switch being unavailingly pressed down because his last act had been to fuse the lights. He judged the moment was right, pulled the twine. No sound had ever been so beautiful as was the crashing noise from above, closely followed by the thuds of regulation boots as they ran up the stairs.

Blackshirt moved with bewildering speed, left the cover of the door, crossed into the nearer room on the right. This was small and square, and had only one window.

He switched on his torch and adjusted the shutters so they were open to their fullest extent, shone it in the direction of the window. Then, he opened the window to the accompaniment of a great deal of noise, stripped off the glove on his left hand. 'Who's there?' he shouted.

Discipline was a two-edge weapon, liable to turn on its user when the disciplinee did not make certain who was the disciplinor. Constable Grasley forgot that, called out, 'It's me.'

'Who the hell is me?'

'Grasley, sir.'

'Get in here and give me a hand.'

Grasley ran up to the window and wished his senior would not shine the light directly in his eyes. He was about to try to climb up without help, when a hand came forward to assist him. He seized hold of it, scrambled up and over the window-sill.

'Who else is on this side with you?'

'Queen, sir.'

'Thanks.' Blackshirt brought his right hand round in an upper-cut that lacked no force because of the short distance it had travelled. Constable Grasley ceased to have any interest in the proceedings.

Blackshirt blew on his knuckles as he crossed to the window. 'Queen,' he shouted.

A second constable ran up. 'Yes, sir.'

'Get inside and join Grasley.'

'Very good, sir.' A hand appeared from beyond the circle of dazzling light, and he gratefully accepted its aid.

'This won't hurt,' said Blackshirt kindly, just before he struck. The second body dropped to the ground.

*

Knight was the first to run down the stairs, but by the time he reached the ground floor two constables had preceded him. They, and the others, slammed their way into the room from which the sound had come.

One constable lay on the floor, still happily unconscious. His companion was trying to stand up but was still too unsteady on his feet to succeed, and he fell back as he made a second plaintive call for help that was again cut short as his rather prominent behind smote the floor.

Knight stared at the two men, then at the open window. His mind, unwilling to comprehend what he saw, told him it was a visual lie. Gradually the knowledge came to him that it was the truth.

From outside came the sound of running feet. A man spoke to them through the open window. 'Anything wrong inside?'

The innocent, and well-meaning, enquiry opened the flood-gates. Knight informed all those about him what was the value of their past services, how he rated their present ones, what the future probably held for them.

Both constables recovered fully, apart from their headaches, and no one showed any desire to sympathize with them over that, and they reluctantly related what had happened. When it became apparent to Knight that his men had all but rushed forward to meet trouble, his sarcasm increased to the point where it was very difficult to know what he was talking about, and only when the twine in the hall was discovered and certain facts were made clear, did his words become less as he realized that he, himself, did not emerge with reputation unsullied.

All that could be said, had been, and Knight knew he could not delay the report any longer. He made it by telephone, and was told to await the arrival of Superintendent Ashley. He felt that life had dealt him all the dirty cards that were in the pack.

Ashley arrived, cigarette attached to upper lip, and politely asked to be told more fully what had happened, then expressed much surprise as the facts were reluctantly explained to him. His attitude was quietly most insulting, and Knight became certain he had never before disliked a man so much.

'Shall we go and see the body?' suggested Ashley.

'It's upstairs.'

'So you said.'

They went upstairs and entered the room in which was Brindle's body.

'Didn't mean him to talk afterwards,' said Knight, hoping to divert the conversation from the channels along which it had been flowing.

'Funny how a man can suddenly change into a killer, isn't it?'

'Probably Blackshirt basically always was one.'

'Until he killed Parlant he was no murderer.' The Superintendent stared at the body. ''Phone HQ. and make a report; ask them to send Hooper out. In the meantime, you might as well dismiss everyone—I don't think they'll be of much use, do you?'

Knight flushed, mumbled something, left the room.

Police routine came to the house of the murdered man, and for a long while the rooms echoed to the sounds of those who dusted, measured, photographed. Eventually the work was done and the men left, and only Ashley, Hooper, and one constable remained.

Hooper offered his cigarette case around and was disheartened when both the other two accepted. 'I'd say this does away with any more ifs and buts,' he announced and indicated where the body had been.

Ashley slowly nodded his head. He sat on a chair, legs crossed, arms folded. The cigarette hung down from his upper lip and the smoke trailed upwards into his eyes, but they seemed to be unaffected.

'I reckon we don't have to argue now about who killed Parlant?'

'You're smart, Bill, real damn' smart.'

Considering the vehemence with which in the past Ashley had denied the possibility of Blackshirt being the murderer of the Judge, and the boring way in which he had produced his dog-eared theories of coincidence, it seemed to Hooper that to make amends the least he could do now was to refrain from sarcasm directed at the Detective-Sergeant.

'It's like having a stoat loose amongst a hutch-full of rabbits,' said the Superintendent suddenly, with what was, for him, an amazing choice of words.

'Any ideas what he's after?'

'Your guess is as good as mine.'

'I haven't got one.'

'No more have I.'

Ashley stared at the wooden floorboards where they were not covered by the well-worn carpet. The blood-stain was large and of ominous shape.

'To think they had him tied up here, then let him slide through their fingers,' he muttered despondently.

'Wonder they didn't escort him out under an archway of raised truncheons.'

'A boy of five could have told them the one about hiding behind a door.' Ashley was suitably indignant, happy in the knowledge that he did not have to ask himself the question of whether he would have seen through the ruse. 'Knight must have been granted a few brains when he was born, yet you certainly wouldn't think that was the case. If you want my opinion, he's not fit to be left in charge of a comatose tortoise. Blackshirt, murderer, bottled up, and what happens?'

'That,' remarked a new voice, 'is not quite so certain as you would seem to think.'

The mental shock of the completely unexpected affected them more than would have physical action. They experienced fear, panic and a frantic desire to hide, in a space of time too short to record. Then their trained minds recovered and forced them to think and act as policemen. Each man turned towards the direction from which the voice had come.

Blackshirt stood in the doorway.

Again they were shocked, but this time the effect was to make their minds doubt that their eyes recorded truly.

'I am neither a murderer, nor did I escape from the house.'

Hooper shrugged aside the strange compulsion to inaction that had fastened about him, a feeling fostered by the ease with which the cracksman stood there and mocked them.

'Don't panic,' said Blackshirt calmly, noticing the sudden tension about the Sergeant.

'Get him, constable,' shouted Hooper, and threw himself forward.

Hooper had a natural flair for unarmed combat, and this, added to the fact that he was of a strong build made of him a most formidable fighter, as many criminals had all too painfully discovered. Indeed, immediately before he slammed his shoulders into the cracksman's side and threw him to the ground, he thought how typical it was that it should be the vanity of the other, who believed he was a match for anyone, that brought him to disaster.

Hooper's mind had, unfortunately, progressed a little ahead of schedule. True, his shoulders should have connected with the other, and the black figure should have crashed to the ground, but somewhere along the line events became mixed up and it was the Detective-Sergeant who flew through the air with little grace but a certain ease, and who smote the floor violently and immediately lost consciousness.

The constable was halfway to battle when he saw the solidly built Hooper handled with consummate ease and casually thrown a few feet to one side. It was quite obvious to the constable that he would be no match for the cracksman, but any hesitation of his was but momentary. He continued forward.

The constable performed a somersault before hitting the far wall with such force that some of the plaster came falling down.

Ashley remained seated. He had reached an age where heroism had given way to realism, and since he estimated that if he tried to give battle he would be thrown even further than had been the constable, he stayed where he was.

'Impulsive,' said Blackshirt, indicating the two unconscious men.

Ashley studied the cracksman. Here, as reality and not as some typewritten report, was the man the police had sought for so many years. Here was the legend presenting himself as fact. . . . Despite his loathing for all murderers, the Superintendent could not repress the feeling of awed admiration that arose within him.

Blackshirt dragged the two men to the centre of the room, secured their arms and legs. That done, he drew up another chair, sat down opposite the Superintendent.

'You think I killed Parlant?'

'Yes.'

'I did not.'

'You were in the house at the time of the murder.'

'Maybe—maybe not until afterwards.'

'You're asking me to believe an amazing coincidence,' said the Superintendent, casually forgetting what he had once told Hooper.

'Why?'

He tried carefully to choose his words. 'You broke into the house, you say to secure a snuff-box. The Judge is then found dead. You are asking me to accept that the murderer was yet another intruder.'

'That's the way it was played.'

'I might, because of what you were, have believed you, Blackshirt—until tonight. Then what? Another murder, and again your presence. Logic refutes the possibility of a second coincidence.'

'Agreed—but suppose this second murder was no coincidence, but was planned to coincide with my presence?'

'By whom?'

'The murderer of Parlant.'

'Why?'

Blackshirt shook his head slowly. 'I don't know.'

Ashley's voice was cold. 'Nor do I.' For a while he had forgotten he was talking to a murderer, and his mind could not see beyond the amazing present, but now he could remember the past and the two men who had been battered to death.

The cracksman noted the change in tone of voice. He leaned forward, spoke eagerly. 'Why do you reckon I stayed behind, in this house?'

'You gave the impression you had escaped, but in fact you remained. In that way you ran no fear of being caught outside, while inside the house became a sanctuary.'

'That is half the truth. The other half is that I wanted to talk to someone in authority.'

'And so?'

'I've been operating quite some time, haven't I?'

'Too long.'

'That's a matter of opinion! During that time I've always played the game according to my rules. Those rules do not include murder.'

'They used not to,' admitted Ashley reluctantly.

'They still don't,' snapped Blackshirt. 'I did not see Parlant until I noticed the blood coming from under the door of his room. When I entered with the butler, he was dead. . . . This evening I broke into this house, spoke to Brindle, then tied him up and gagged him. I left him alive. When I returned he was dead.'

Ashley flicked the cigarette butt away from his lips with his tongue. It fell to the floor and he stamped on it. 'You admit to tying him up, yet claim another killed him?'

Blackshirt spoke uneasily, knowing how absurd his words could sound. 'The improbable can happen.'

'It didn't in this case.'

He stared at the Superintendent and within him was an impotent anger. The other was no fool, yet he blindly preferred to decide the cracksman was a murderer rather than listen to reason. . . . Blackshirt relaxed slightly. Since he, himself, also was no fool, he could appreciate how the events would appear as seen by the Superintendent. Quite suddenly a surge of hopelessness swept over him. Whom could he ever hope to find to believe him?

He made one more attempt to prove himself. 'How did the police know I was here?'

'A tip-off.'

'Who gave it?'

'How should I know?'

Blackshirt spoke slowly. 'Would I have given the alarm, placed myself in danger? Did Brindle—dead? Who's left? Only the murderer, who wanted to trap me, lay the murder he committed on me.'

For a moment, it seemed as though the Superintendent might appreciate the worth of those words, but then he shrugged them aside. 'You're clever enough to have made the call yourself, knowing you could escape, and could then come back and try to justify yourself by these same arguments.'

It was useless to argue further. Blackshirt spoke wearily. 'Do I have to tie you up and gag you to ensure my own departure is uneventful?'

The Superintendent shook his head. 'I'll not move—my health's too precious to me.'

'Right now,' snapped the cracksman, 'your health is in a tricky position. Brand me too successfully as a murderer and maybe I'll become eager to prove you're right.'

Ashley shivered. It seemed as though his life insurance policy was about to become due.

Blackshirt left. Hooper and the constable, both of whom had recovered consciousness, waited for Ashley to release them. They waited a long while. The Superintendent was deep in thought.

Chapter Five

ROBERTS sat down in an armchair, accepted a gin and tonic and a cigarette.

Verrell poured himself out a similar drink, then relaxed in another chair, crossed his legs. 'Cheers!'

They drank. The only sound to disturb the peace was the murmur of sound that was the traffic beyond the flat, but the noise was sufficiently dulled that it became merely a pleasant reminder of the outside world.

Verrell blew out cigarette smoke in a series of rings. 'It's a stinking mess,' he said without any preamble.

Roberts stared at his glass, watched the bubbles chasing one another to the surface. 'Is it worse than before, sir?'

'I reckon, yes. In some quarters my reputation saved me from being considered a murderer when I discovered Parlant's body. Blackshirt wouldn't kill, no matter what it might seem. But now that I've been intimately connected with a second murder my reputation must, of necessity, perform a *volte-face*. Blackshirt has beome a disciple of the Borgias.'

'What happened last night?'

'I walked straight into the trap like a good little mouse, and only quick thinking and a huge slice of luck saved me from extinction.'

'The trap must have been well baited.'

Verrell finished his drink, considered the empty glass, stood up, mixed himself a second one. 'There was a touch of brilliance about the entire affair. What bait would be most likely to make Blackshirt come running? Obviously, a report of the cracksman's movements when the real Blackshirt knew it had not been he. The murderer knew this could be guaranteed to bring me in, eager to discover who was taking my name in vain. . . . He did what all good strategists do: he placed himself in the position of his opponent.'

Roberts looked at Verrell. 'Did you have no warning of what was to come?'

'Something about the attitude of Brindle struck me as inconsistent with his character as I judged it, but not sufficiently that I stopped to find out the reason.'

Roberts finished his drink, refused the offer of another. He carefully stubbed out his cigarette in an ashtray. 'What now, sir?'

'Stranded in the middle of a fog, unable to see the alternative routes, of which in any case I don't know the one I require, I'm rather lost.'

'Have you no leads?'

'None.'

Verrell finished the contents of his glass, thought about a third drink, decided it would spoil his lunch, which, to compensate for all that had gone wrong, was to be of noble quality.

'Why did the man choose the home of Brindle?' asked Roberts after a lengthy silence.

'You've picked out the one remote possibility. There must have been some good reason. All we've got to do is discover what it was!'

'Anything to do with the house?'

'All those Victorian barracks are essentially like peas in a pod, and the age was much too pedestrian to have encompassed the thought of secret passages. Besides, there was no need for the murderer to hide too deeply. I wasn't expecting him so his was the immediate advantage.'

'The district?'

'Representative of a dozen others, alike in its positioning to the centre of London and its air of Subtopia.'

Once again they became silent. Verrell wondered what the Superintendent was doing, thought he was probably making life hell for his juniors as he tried to land the biggest fish of his career—Blackshirt, the murderer.

'The law?' asked Roberts suddenly.

'What law?' For the moment Verrell could not understand the sense of the words.

'Both Brindle and the Judge were in law.'

Verrell stubbed out his cigarette, used the stub to draw in the ash. He realized he had pictured a gallows, hastily rubbed the ash into confusion. 'Bit of a different scale.'

'They may not have been social acquaintances, but could easily have been professional ones.'

'I doubt a judge of the High Court has much to do with solicitors.'

'Maybe not, sir, but what about the time before Parlant was a judge? As silk, he had to be briefed.'

'I wonder,' said Verrell slowly. The more he considered the possibility, the better it made sense. Previously he had tried to find the connection between the two murders and had failed. This was something he had overlooked. 'Could be that the murderer had trade to do with both of them, and decided to kill two birds with one stone.'

'Something that arose because of the relationship of barrister, solicitor, and client?'

'The client had to find out something, hence the torture to which the Judge was subjected before he was killed. . . . How long since the Judge was raised to the Bench, Roberts?'

'I don't know, sir, off-hand.'

'Care to find out?'

Roberts rose from the chair, left the room. Verrell relaxed slightly. So far he had been unable to find anything, or anyone, against whom he could fight. Now it seemed there might be a chance the picture would change.

The connection was, so far, a most tenuous one. The two murdered men had both been attached to the law, and that was all, and normally he would have thought the matter a coincidence. But because he needed something, some fact, to work on, he accepted the connection as more than fortuitous, and pondered on what it could mean.

Roberts returned to the room. 'Sir Ernest Parlant was made a judge six years ago.'

The trail, then, was an old one. Six years was a long time in the criminal world. Enmities would be forgotten, new alliances made. Six years, or more, was a long time to wait for revenge . . . Unless prison walls had forced the wait, had fostered and increased the hatred. 'We've got to track back, Roberts, find out what cases Parlant handled before he went on the Bench.'

'That's what I was thinking, sir.'

'Maybe we can flush a conspiracy—something tells me there's a mint of money at stake.'

'A judge mixed up in a conspiracy?' asked Roberts, horrified by the suggestion.

'If we're right, he was only silk at the time.' But Verrell spoke uncertainly, since counsel was like Caesar's wife. Yet who was to testify how she behaved when Caesar was not at home?

*

Roberts dressed with immaculate precision, and endowed himself with great respectability. A bowler hat negated any form of skulduggery, and rolled umbrella, with silver embossed handle, made fraud an unthinkable word. No matter what the circumstances, no policeman would have ever dared suggest that Roberts was acting suspiciously.

He climbed the six steps which led up to the small landing and studied the names printed on the door on his right. He was disagreeably surprised by the seedy atmosphere of the building which housed several sets of chambers.

Sir Ernest Parlant's name was at the top of the list, and although an effort had been made to cover over the name with a strip of cardboard, this had fallen away and hung straight downwards, supported by the remaining tack.

There was a notice requesting him to knock and enter; this he did, carefully closing the door behind him.

He was in a corridor into which little natural light was allowed to filter, and it was with difficulty that he read the words, "Clerks' Room," on the door to his left. As he went to walk forward, this door opened, and a young man, noticeable for his draped coat with velvet collar and his string tie, looked out. 'Yus?'

Roberts felt that the majesty of the law demanded better than this, and there was marked disapproval in his voice as he asked to speak to the chief clerk. The boy vanished from sight, reappeared a few seconds later and flung the door open to its fullest extent.

The chief clerk rose from a chair. The building was obviously very old, and it now seemed not unreasonable to suppose that the clerk had first begun work as soon as it was built. He was a small man, whom age had made smaller, and were it not for the expression in his eyes might have been mistaken for an example of the embalmer's art. The eyes were sharp and bright.

'Can I help you?' he asked.

'I should much appreciate a word with you,' replied Roberts, equally non-committally polite.

'You are from?'

'A newspaper.'

The chief clerk returned to his chair and sat down. Excess politeness was shown only to solicitors and their clerks. 'What did you want to know?'

'Something about Mr. Justice Parlant.' Roberts looked around the room. Bundles of papers, tied with red ribbon, lay everywhere. The young man sat at a desk on which was a small inter-office telephone switchboard, and audibly chewed gum. At the third desk a woman of indeterminate age peered shortsightedly at a sheet of handwriting she was trying to decipher.

'What about him?' asked the clerk.

'We are thinking of doing a series, based on the cases he was connected with, both as a silk and as judge.'

The chief clerk spoke coldly. 'I don't think I can help you.'

'Name his big cases and we can do the rest.'

'I couldn't possibly act in such manner. Any information I might have is strictly confidential.'

'Any money in it?' asked the youth.

'Might be,' replied Roberts. Since meeting the chief clerk he had rated at nil the chances of a successful conclusion to his mission.

'How much?' demanded the youth.

'Be quiet, Edwin,' ordered the chief clerk.

'What's wrong with making ourselves a quick handful of folding money?'

The chief clerk shivered slightly, and his eyes expressed sadness. In his day not only was English spoken, it was also not spoken by juniors until they were spoken to. He addressed Roberts. 'We cannot give you the information you desire.'

'Sorry about that,' answered Roberts.

'Edwin, show the gentleman out.'

The youth hastened to do as he was bid, and it came as no surprise when a hurried enquiry was made at the outside door as to whether he, Edwin, could be of any assistance.

*

'Not talking?' asked Verrell.

'No, sir.'

'Pity!' Verrell grinned. He had broken into many places, but never before a set of chambers.

*

The Temple was a succession of small deserted squares more attractive in the darkness than by day, since the size of the buildings lent an air of majesty, and the details of their architecture was, for the most part, hidden.

Verrell reached the entrance of the building in which were the chambers of the late Mr. Justice Parlant. All was quiet, and he had seen no one since he had entered the Temple. He made one last check, went in.

He removed his white scarf, donned black gloves and hood, crossed to the heavy wooden door on his right. This was shut, so that the names of the occupants of the chambers no longer showed. He studied the lock, took an adjustable key from his belt of tools and inserted it. When he twisted, the tumblers of the lock half-turned, then stuck. He withdrew the key, altered the setting, tried again. The lock clicked open.

He swung the door back, and immediately in front of him was another one. The second lock was of the Yale type, and using a strip of mica he forced it at once.

Blackshirt entered the corridor, closed the two doors behind him. He turned left and went into the clerks' room.

To Roberts, the room had appeared untidy; to Blackshirt, who had to search through it, it was in a shambles. Reluctantly, he started in one corner and began to check. He slowly made his way through a flood of briefs, some marked with the fees, some unmarked, some new, some dated years before; through files of carbon copies of pleadings; through drawers filled with the products of fifty years during which time nothing that might one day be of use had been thrown away. Eventually, only a tin box underneath the clerk's desk remained to be examined.

The lock of the box was recalcitrant. It was of simple design, but being old and almost worn out, acted in an illogical and annoying manner. Beneath his hood, Blackshirt grinned. It was defying his efforts to open it because it was in a condition into which it should never have been allowed to get.

None of his skeleton keys would turn the tumblers, nor would any of the pick-like instruments. He inserted a very thin rod of steel into the lock, tapped the end of the rod with his clenched fist. Locks could become almost human in the way in which they would respond to nothing but force. He struck twice and there was a "click." He tried to lift the lid, but it was still secure, so he shifted the point of the rod, struck again, and this time had the satisfaction of feeling the tumblers slide back. At the same moment he heard a sound from the passage beyond.

There had been no more than a sigh of noise, such as would leave the normal listener, even should he catch it, certain he had heard nothing when the sound was not repeated.

Blackshirt waited, motionless. Again came the whisper of movement. He left the lighted torch where it was, and rose to his feet, then leaned on the desk and opened one of the briefs. His left hand was hidden by his body: he reached to his belt and took from it a small mirror which he held in position.

There was so little light he could but dimly make out the figure in the doorway. He continued to appear to read.

The man took a step forward.

Blackshirt shifted his balance until he could move instantly. He had noted two facts. The man was dressed in something dark: in his right hand was metal that glinted in the poor light given by the torch.

The man lunged forward, right arm extended. Blackshirt twisted to one side, and the knife sliced the air two inches beyond him. He whipped round, faced his assailant.

The killer's face was hidden by a black hood; he wore a black shirt. It was Blackshirt seeking to kill Blackshirt.

The man flashed knife from right hand to left, jabbed sideways. To avoid the stroke, Blackshirt was forced to draw back until he was against the desk. There could be no further retreat.

There was another sharp lunge, then the knife was thrown back to the right hand even as that lunge failed: a circular sweep, and a quick spasm of pain pierced Blackshirt's side. First blood had been drawn.

The man who opposed Blackshirt was an expert knife-fighter—so much had become obvious at once. Such being the case, unless he, Blackshirt, could break free almost immediately he would be dead—the enclosed space gave all the advantage to the other man. The knife began to flash towards Blackshirt. He altered his balance, swayed, and once more the knife missed his side. He swept his right hand downwards and caught the wrist of the other, jerked forwards, tried to kick the man's feet away from under him.

He only partially succeeded, since his opponent twisted sufficiently to retain balance, yet there was a short space of time in which he could move without danger and which enabled him to get clear of the desk. He breathed more freely. The odds against him had become less overwhelming.

The man tried to drag his arm free from Blackshirt's grip, failed, suddenly flicked the knife across to his left hand, lashed out. Blackshirt threw himself forward so that he came within the arc of the blow, wrapped himself about the other, heaved backwards, suddenly changed the direction of force so that he pushed, again kicked the inside of his opponent's legs. This time the two men crashed to the ground.

Blackshirt secured an arm lock. A fist crashed into the side of his head; he ignored the pain, increased the force of the lock. For a brief moment the other resisted, then the agony became too great. With a gasp that was almost a cry he let go of the knife. The murderer was afraid. Never before had he been worsted, yet now it had happened at the hands of an unarmed man. He felt the hold on his arm slackening slightly, jerked it free, rolled away, rose to his feet and plunged towards the doorway from which he had so recently come, certain he would kill.

Blackshirt had not expected the fight to end suddenly and had been concentrating on the knife rather than the immediate intentions of his opponent. He was not prepared for the other to attempt to escape, could do nothing to prevent it. His fault had been to endow the murderer with more fighting spirit than he possessed.

Blackshirt drew up his shirt and examined the wound in his side. The knife had parted the flesh cleanly, and although a certain amount of blood had been lost, the wound was now dry. He tucked his shirt back inside his trousers.

It was possible that the murderer would sound the alarm, but was not probable. Blackshirt judged it safe to reckon all would remain quiet. He lifted the lid of the steel box, examined the contents.

There was a cash box, empty of money but containing several I.O.U.s for varying amounts, several books of cheque-stubs, a one ounce packet of stale tobacco, a highly confidential book which Blackshirt examined and found to be filled with private, and in many cases highly derogatory, details of the solicitors with whom chambers dealt, and finally, that for which he sought. Two dozen counsel's fees books, some new and clean, some old and dusty.

Blackshirt checked through the book which listed the fees of Mr. Ernest Parlant, and was astonished to discover what that gentleman was earning immediately before he became a Judge. Evidently, not every counsel at the Bar was near the bread-line. In the same line as was the note of the fee paid, there was also the name of the case and that of the briefing solicitor. Blackshirt realized he did not know for which firm Brindle had worked, checked in the Law List that was on top of the desk. He then referred back to the fee book and noted the cases in which that firm of solicitors were briefing. In a very short while he realized that, unaided, he would get nowhere. He looked up, and almost immediately in front of him was a list of addresses. It seemed in the nature of an omen.

*

Mr. Tolby, chief clerk, slept in a nightgown. That fact was the skeleton in his cupboard; even to his thoughts the subject was taboo. He lived with his married daughter, had done since the death of his wife, and not even she was aware of the nature of his garment of repose. It would have been sacrilege to mention it, unthinkable that she should ever see it. Therefore, when Mr. Tolby was awoken by a brisk shake of the shoulders, his first instinct was to run because the house must be on fire; his second, to secure the bed-clothes more firmly about his neck so that none might see that which must remain hidden.

He opened his eyes, and since he needed spectacles only for reading or writing, could quite clearly make out the figure in black.

'Sorry to trouble you,' said Blackshirt politely.

Mr. Tolby trembled slightly. 'What do you want? Go away. How dare you!'

'Mind if I sit down?'

'I shall call the police.'

'How?'

'You're Blackshirt, aren't you?'

He nodded.

'It's no good battering me to death,' declared Mr. Tolby, 'I haven't got anything worth while. You'd better go and try someone else.' He was greatly frightened, but men of his generation never admitted to such thing.

Blackshirt regarded him with affection. He admired a fighter, never more so than when such person knew the position to be hopeless. 'There's no need to panic—all I want to do is to ask you a few questions.'

'I shall answer nothing.'

'I want you to tell me about some of these cases.' He lifted up the fee book he carried.

'How did you get that? You've stolen it,' accused Mr. Tolby indignantly.

Blackshirt admitted that that was so.

'It's outrageous. That book is confidential and no unauthorized person is allowed to see it. How dare you act in such a despicable manner.'

Blackshirt coughed.

'Kindly give me back that book and then leave.'

Blackshirt decided certain facts must be made clear. 'I've been to a great deal of trouble and suffered not a little danger to secure this book. I was all but knifed, spent a long time opening your tin box, then had to "borrow" a car to make my way out to this part of London, which I must confess I thought until now only existed in the books by *avant-garde* writers.'

'I've no idea what you are talking about, but nothing you can do or say will make me speak.' Mr. Tolby's expression assumed that of a martyr, glad to be dying for the cause, but regretful that the path to be trodden had to be quite so thorny.

'Nothing?'

'If you think that by bashing in my head like you did those others you'll make me speak, you're very much mistaken.'

Blackshirt thought that such logic was unassailable. He wondered how to break down such determined resistance and had decided he would be unable to, when he noticed something. Mr. Tolby still held the bed-clothes tightly about him. Blackshirt wondered if the sudden spurt of inspiration within himself could possibly be correct. He sat down on the bed. 'Cold?' he asked kindly.

'No.'

'I was wondering why you clutched sheet and blankets so tightly about yourself.'

Fear came to Mr. Tolby. 'I. . . . Yes, I am a little chilly.'

'The night's warm.'

'I suffer from a slight cold.'

Without warning, Blackshirt ripped the bed-clothes away from the other.

Mr. Tolby quivered, frantically tried to hide himself.

'Haven't seen a nightgown like that outside a museum. . . . Such an attractive colour.'

Mr. Tolby read the most awful threats into those apparently innocuous words. He saw his nightgown floating from a masthead so that all the neighbours could see it: he saw the taboo broken, the ridicule, the scorn.

As he watched the other's tortured expression, Blackshirt felt certain he had never been guilty of a more despicable action. He tried to bring some relief to the unfortunate man. 'I need the information from you to help me discover who did kill the Judge.'

'Didn't you?'

'No.'

'The papers . . .'

'Lies.'

Mr. Tolby at last felt that there might be justification for what he was going to do, and being the man he was, decided he might speak, subject to one qualification. 'What I say will be highly confidential.'

'I shall treat it as such.'

He waited for the questions.

*

Blackshirt sat in the car and wondered where he went from there. What he had learned from the chief clerk had been no help. Mr. Tolby, with the partitioned memory so commonly found, had been able to say whether each case had been won or lost, where it had taken place, and how soon the cheque was paid by the briefing solicitors, but could rarely remember the details: those, to him, were of no importance. Blackshirt stared through the windscreen of the car. It was as near certain as anything unproved could be, that hidden within the book he had was the answer, or part of it, to the murders of the Judge and Brindle. Were that not so, there would not have been an attempt on his life in the chambers. The assailant had come to destroy the evidence, knowing that as Blackshirt had not been caught by the police at Brindle's home, soon he must realize the connection between the men of law and try to trace its meaning.

How to translate what was written in the book? Was there anyone but the murderer who could do such translating?

He thought of Otto, decided the other might be able to assist. He pressed the starter button on the car, and the engine whispered into life. Blackshirt had good taste, and when he "borrowed" a car, he always made certain it was one of the better makes, unless the work he expected to give it was likely to be on the rough side. He would never willingly ill-treat a good car.

He drove away from the pavement, decided that Otto would be annoyed at being wakened up. He smiled.

*

Otto Speyer was very annoyed, but he kept that annoyance to himself. Being the largest fence in London, a position he maintained by means of blackmail, thuggery, bribery and wholesale corruption, he normally feared no one, but all feared him. Yet because he did not know the identity of Blackshirt, and the cracksman knew him for what he was, he feared the other.

'Hope I didn't disturb you,' said Blackshirt.

Since Speyer had been asleep for several hours and, but for the intrusion, would obviously have remained thus for several more, he felt the words were extremely hypocritical.

'I sometimes think you sleep much too much for the good of your health.'

Speyer wished he had had a trapdoor built in the floor of his bedroom: one of those that gave immediate access to large steel spikes stuck vertically upwards.

'Can I pour you out a drink?'

For the first time Blackshirt spoke sense, and Speyer replied that the other could do as was suggested. The fence sat up, wedged two pillows behind his back, and waited impatiently until the glass was handed to him. He drank the contents in a remarkably short time, held out the empty glass in an unmistakable gesture. It was refilled. This time he drank more slowly. He lit a cigarette, stared at the cracksman, noticed he was observed, hurriedly looked away.

'No,' snapped Blackshirt, and his voice was harsh.

'No what?'

'I didn't kill them.'

Speyer reddened. 'Never thought you did.' This was hardly true. The cracksman's philosophy of life was so different to his own, he had never really understood or believed it; the report of the two murders had convinced him that Blackshirt's true nature was at last exposed, and since it proved to be remarkably similar to those possessed by the people with whom Speyer normally dealt, the fence had felt that all was in order.

'Think I'm a liar?' asked Blackshirt.

'Of course not. Not for one moment did I believe a word of what I read.'

'Bet you had a good try.'

Speyer wished his visitor to worse deaths than steel spikes, finished his drink, knew—and this angered him—that should he ever receive the news of Blackshirt's death he would feel he had lost a friend. The paradoxical relationship that existed between the two men would have surprised anyone who did not know them both very well. 'What happened, Blackshirt?'

The full story was told clearly and concisely.

'He's been clever,' was what the fence said at the conclusion.

'Damn' nearly too clever for my health. One slice less of luck, and I would have been a goner.'

'Have you no lead?'

'I don't know.' Blackshirt laid the counsel's fee book on the bed, opened it. 'There's some form of connection between the two murders, Otto, and I'll stake everything that it can be found in this book—if you know the language. There are a number of entries here, covering several years, of the cases in which Brindle's firm briefed Parlant. I've gone through them, but so far have discovered nothing to cause excitement. I'm wondering if you can do better.'

'It's a hell of a thick book,' grumbled Speyer. 'What could I possibly know about any of them?'

'A silk of Parlant's standing only takes on a criminal case when there's big money or good publicity involved—that adds up to the fact that all the cases in here will be big ones, and you'll know them.'

'I doubt it. Anyway, you know as much as me.'

Blackshirt opened the book and, not heeding the obvious reluctance of the other, read out the names of the criminal cases in which Parlant had been briefed by Brindle's firm.

Sometimes Speyer remembered the case immediately, could recall the details and names of all the men concerned; at other times he had to think back a long while before he could gain the slightest recollection.

Blackshirt read out name after name.

'George Weit?'

'Weit . . . Weit . . . What year?' asked Speyer, now drinking his fifth whisky.

'Same as before, six weeks later.'

He lit another cigarette. 'It was either a bank job or a wages snatch. Which the hell was it?'

Blackshirt uncrossed his legs, crossed them over the opposite way. He looked at the clock in the far corner of the room and noted how little time there was until dawn.

'Weit got something like four years, and his late partners vanished along with the money as soon as he was safely inside.'

'What happened to the money?'

'Not knowing, can't say.' Speyer shifted the pillows behind his back until they no longer supported his head. If he were forced to hold his head upright, he was less likely to fall asleep.

'Was it much?'

'Maybe a couple of thousand.' Speyer was uninterested in thefts of money; men did not come to him to sell it.

Blackshirt sighed, turned over a page. They had almost reached the end of the book and had discovered nothing. Should they continue to fail, he could not see what his next move could be. He read out the next name. 'Albert Blair.'

Speyer rubbed his eyes. 'You can't need me to tell you the history of that one.'

'Doesn't say anything to me.'

'If you never once thought about helping yourself to the Milton Cross, I'll take up stone-breaking in a prison quarry.'

'The Milton Cross,' said Blackshirt slowly.

Speyer stubbed out his cigarette, lit another. He knew smoking was said to be bad for his health, but so was drinking, and if one cut out those two enjoyments, what was left to life?

Blackshirt stood up, paced slowly backwards and forwards across the room. 'My memory's ticking over at last. . . . I was abroad and it was difficult to buy English newspapers. I only read about the theft of the Cross a week after it had happened.'

The man in bed made no comment.

'Wasn't a bad little haul, was it?'

'Little? Blackshirt, not even you can refer to those diamonds in such words. I examined the Cross when it was exhibited, and the diamonds were the most beautiful I have seen. They were flawless. I longed to cradle them in my hand, gain the exquisite pleasure of physical contact.'

'Which I expect you did after Blair was forced to sell them to you at a tenth of their real value.'

'You don't remember!' Speyer finished the contents of his glass, indicated he was still thirsty. The cracksman ceased pacing the floor, poured out the drink, handed it to the fence.

'Blair,' continued Speyer, 'carried out a burglary of which you, Blackshirt, would not have been ashamed. It was planned with precision and a marvellous eye to detail, and because of this it succeeded. The value of the haul was tens of thousands according to some, hundreds of thousands according to others. Myself, I should say the Cross was worth one hundred and fifty thousand pounds.'

'Then I'll accept that figure.'

'Blair took the Cross, and should have been sitting pretty. But he wasn't like you, Blackshirt, ready to be content: two weeks later, he saw a chance to make himself another few thousand pounds, and took it. He ended in jail.'

Blackshirt sat down on the bed. 'What happened to the Cross?'

Speyer shook his head. 'Your guess is as good as mine. At first the police didn't know whom they'd caught. Then the whisper must have gone round, because they connected Blair up with the Milton Cross job, even though they couldn't prove anything. They offered him a hell of a lot if he'd tell them what he'd done with the Cross, but he just laughed. They never did find a trace of it.'

'He's out now?'

'Depends what you mean by out.' Speyer was excited. Quite suddenly he realized what his words meant. 'He received a hell of a sentence because his record was a yard long and because he refused to help the police. Not long after he went inside he made a break for it.'

Blackshirt remembered the rest of the story. Blair had planned brilliantly, executed his escape exactly; then luck had run out on him. The stolen car in which he was making his getaway had crashed down the side of a gulley that lay beyond the corner of the road he had tried to take at too great a speed. The car had burned out and the police found little beyond cinders.

'What happened to the Cross?' asked Blackshirt, for the second time.

'Remained vanished.'

He spoke slowly. 'That's the bait now.'

'Reckon you're right, Blackshirt.'

Beneath the hood the features of the cracksman relaxed slightly. One at least of the questions had been answered.

Chapter Six

BLACKSHIRT slowly drove the car back to where he would leave it. His eyes noted the road ahead, his hands adjusted the turn of the steering wheel, his feet were ready to depress clutch or brake pedal; yet his mind considered nothing but the Milton Cross.

He did not see the Cross as it was, thirteen diamonds in beautifully chased gold setting, nor did he visualize it in words; his thoughts were a mixture of words and images, where one became the other.

At one point he told himself that he might not have reached the correct solution—that the murderer was not after the Cross. Then he dismissed such suggestion. Diamonds worth between one and two hundred thousand pounds were the most persuasive bait there could be—bait that would provoke murder after murder.

The Judge had been tortured to make him reveal the whereabouts of the jewels, then killed. Had he been able to give the information that was demanded? Brindle, the solicitor, had been killed because of the jewels. Either Brindle had had them, and not the Judge, or else they had both had some. What had been divided once might be so again.

He, Blackshirt, had to trace the jewels. It was no use saying it was too late, that there was nothing to guide him, that the task was an impossibility. He had to trace them, because otherwise Blackshirt would remain branded a murderer. . . .

The struggle was for the Milton Cross, stolen by Blair, whereabouts unknown.

Where and how did he try to uncover the past? Speyer could tell him nothing, which was tantamount to saying no one could. If Speyer could not trace the information, no one else was likely to succeed.

Had he any leads to follow? That depended on what one called a lead. By normal standards he had not. Yet one thing gave him hope: there was still plenty of fight. The murderer had tried to prevent his knowing that the Milton Cross was the bait. Had the other obtained it by now, there would be little point in having gone to such lengths to prevent that information becoming known to Blackshirt. Therefore it seemed reasonable to suppose

61

that the murderer had not yet secured the Cross. Which meant that Blackshirt still had a chance to prove it was not he who had killed.

Subconsciously he noted that he was returning to the road from which he had taken the car, and he forced his mind back to the immediate present. He checked that all was quiet, brought the car to a halt, left it, locked the door behind him.

He walked along the pavement with the attitude of one who knew he led a blameless life and was ready to prove such fact to any patrolling constable who doubted it. No constable, seeing him, would have dared to doubt.

*

Superintendent Ashley attached the cigarette to his lip, struck a match, allowed the match to burn itself out. He sighed deeply, wondered why life had to treat him so harshly when he had reached an age at which peace was the prime requisite.

On the table before him were three files and one map. There was a file for each of the two murdered men, and one for Blackshirt. This last was an affectation, demonstrably so when one opened it. Inside was nothing. The map was London and had half a dozen flags stuck in it. Ashley was a great flag-sticker, and never conducted a case without a supply of pins and cardboard.

He wondered what Simpson, the Assistant Commissioner, would say to a few frank words. No man was a miracle worker, no man could do the impossible. Why, then, castigate a poor hard-working Superintendent for not catching Blackshirt at the first, or even second, attempt? Ashley sighed loudly. Simpson was not the man to view matters in so logical a light.

He looked at his watch. It was time for coffee, but since Hooper was out somewhere, and everyone else was incapable of making a cup of coffee that was even remotely drinkable, he, Ashley, would have to go thirsty. Was it to be treated thus, he asked himself sourly, that he had been promoted to his present high position?

He thought about Blackshirt. For many years, and in company with others whose job it had been to try and catch the impudent cracksman, he had had an active regard for Blackshirt. The police loathed the average major criminal because he, or she, was a person who was mean of thought, brutal of action. Blackshirt had been cast from a different mould. He fought with his wits, not weapons, chose the difficult course if it afforded him more amusement, and pursued with pleasure his personal challenge

62

against the police force for the excitement it gave him. One had to admire such a character, even when one suffered the results of the cracksman's over-enthusiastic sense of humour. In direct contrast, Blackshirt the murderer one could not but detest, become determined to stamp him out from the stream of humanity.

Ashley knew that it was because of Blackshirt that he, the Superintendent, was right then going without coffee. It added a sense of personal hate to the proceedings.

Something became crystal clear. If he didn't have his coffee soon, he'd die of thirst.

He left his room, entered the one next to it, spoke to the constable therein. He returned, sat down behind his desk, and waited.

A quarter of an hour later the constable knocked on the door and entered. He carried a cup of coffee in his hands.

'No saucer?' grumbled Ashley.

'Didn't know you wanted one, sir.'

'Think I was born in the wilds of Africa?' he demanded, had the misfortune to look at the constable's face at that moment and realize what was the answer to his question.

'Sorry, sir.'

Ashley mumbled to himself, and the pause gave the constable a chance to leave.

The coffee tasted as it looked, which was very unfortunate, and the fact that a small black insect, very dead, was floating on the surface seemed nothing more than appropriate.

Detective-Sergeant Hooper entered the room. 'Ye gods, I've had a hell of a time,' he announced.

'To hell with the sob story.'

'You sound narked,' he said unwisely.

The Superintendent let it be known, quite unambiguously, that a superior did not expect to be addressed in such manner by an inferior, especially when coffee had been undrinkable.

Hooper began to feel most aggrieved. He had come looking for sympathy, not insults.

'What happened?' demanded Ashley, at length recalling the fact that the Sergeant had returned from a job of work.

'I saw this chap Tolby. He's a refugee from the Napoleonic Wars.'

'Could we stick to the facts?'

'I think that matters.'

'Then it undoubtedly doesn't.'

Hooper hummed a tune to himself that expressed much of what he wanted to say. 'I called in at the chambers, sir, and investigated the damage there.'

'Which was?'

'The tin box they call a safe had been broken open and one of the books taken.'

'What kind of a book?'

'A record of brief fees of Mr. Ernest Parlant when he was practising at the Bar. . . . The Clerk never throws a thing away, and he'd kept this book when the old boy was made a judge, and apparently hadn't even thought of throwing it away after the murder.'

'Is that all that was gone?'

'Yes.' Hooper waited to see if there would be any further questions, but there were none. 'Something else of interest, though.'

'Such as?'

'Couple of stains on the floor that might be blood—they're testing them at the lab, now.'

'Blood? What the hell does that mean?'

'You ask me.'

'I am, dammit.'

'Then I don't know, sir.' Hooper spoke in the flat voice that denoted he was more concerned with his thoughts than his words. 'I checked thoroughly, and am prepared to bet Blackshirt didn't cut himself on anything in the room. Must have done it on something he was carrying.'

'Why?'

'These things happen.'

'Yes,' grunted Ashley. He visualized this room he had never seen. He tried to picture Blackshirt cutting himself on a chisel, but things didn't match up. An expert could, exceptionally, make the mistake of a tyro, but . . . Unbidden, another picture formed in his mind. Two men fought. 'D'you think——?' he began. He stopped. Almost he had made a fool of himself.

'Yes?'

'Nothing.' He realized the cigarette was still firmly attached to his lip and searched for a box of matches. He remembered moving the cigarette in order to drink the liquid that disgraced the name of coffee, but could not remember replacing it, unlit. He struck a match, inhaled smoke, blew it out. 'What about the clerk?'

'He's a rum one.'

'So you've already said a dozen times. What d'you learn from him?'

'Nothing we didn't already know from the report. He woke up and there was Blackshirt. Said it nearly gave him a turn.'

'Just forget the medical history. What did Blackshirt want?'

'A report on the cases in the fee book he'd taken from chambers—those in which Brindle had briefed Parlant when the latter was silk.'

The Superintendent knocked the ash from the end of his cigarette, picked up a pencil and played with it in his fingers. 'What were those cases?'

'Clerk can't remember half of them.'

'No duplicate list?'

'None—— but it may not matter too much.'

The pencil in Ashley's fingers became momentarily still. He leaned across his desk until the edge pressed into his stomach. 'Why not?' he demanded, and his voice was harsh.

'Amongst those he did remember and told me about was the Blair job.'

'Blair . . . Blair?' The Superintendent could not switch the direction of his mind quickly enough, and for a brief moment his memory refused to function.

'The Milton Cross.'

'Well, I'll be jiggered!' He let out his breath in a long hiss of excitement. He dropped the pencil, took the cigarette from his lips and stubbed it out in the dregs of the coffee. 'Bill, we're getting somewhere at last,' he said loudly. 'That's what the stakes are—a fortune in diamonds.'

'Looks like it, though of course, we can't be certain.'

'Care to bet on it?'

'Never bet.'

'Realize something else, Bill?'

'Give it a name.'

'Blackshirt was searching, trying to find what lay behind the murders. Why else did he break into the chambers, then go down and see the clerk fellow?'

'So?' asked Hooper, a trifle belligerently.

'If he didn't know what he was after, would he have beaten up the Judge to find it?'

'Yes, if he were trying to find out what it was he was searching for.'

It was a narrow point that Ashley did not pursue. His mind returned to more important things. 'Go down and get hold of the records on the Blair case, Bill. Maybe they'll give us some fresh ideas.' He waited until the other was at the door. 'And while you're about it, brew up another cup of coffee, would you?'

*

'Since,' said Verrell slowly, 'he tried to prevent my obtaining the lead through to the Blair case, he has not yet obtained the Cross.'

Roberts thought for a while before answering. 'Is that certain, sir?'

'There are objections to the proposition, but I don't think they're valid ones. When both the solicitor and Judge were murdered, we reckoned there must be a connection between them and the law. There was, and it led to the Milton Cross. If the murderer were merely worried about my knowing that much, he need not have tried to kill me in chambers. That fact, by itself, merely takes us back along the path we've just travelled—back to the Judge, the solicitor and the law. It was because it led further the murderer tried to act.' Verrell touched the side of his chest where the knife had sliced the flesh. The wound had completely closed and was now itching.

'Maybe, sir.'

'You're still doubtful?' He turned and looked out of the window, watched an aeroplane high in the sky glint as the sunlight was reflected from its wings. 'If I'm wrong, we're at the end of the line and there's nothing more we can do.'

Roberts grinned. 'Knowing you, sir, I take back everything. I'd hate to spoil the fun.'

'Fun?' For once, Verrell's face set in harsh lines and the expression in his eyes was angry, threatening. 'If I don't succeed I'm branded as a murderer. After that, if ever I'm unlucky enough to be caught it'll be a capital charge they slap on me.'

'The police may have discovered sufficient of the truth by now to know you didn't kill.'

'Unfortunately they have been long convinced they know all of the truth and they've named me the murderer—which means all their investigations are falsely coloured.'

Roberts was silent. He realized how futile would be any further efforts to cheer up the other.

Verrell's mood changed. 'Let's try to clear up a few of the loose ends. The Judge is tortured, then killed. Because of the extent of that torture I'm going to presume that he did not, or could not, say what it was the murderer wanted to know. Next, an effort is made to trap me, and for this purpose Brindle is the bait—subsequently to be killed. He was not tortured. This means he gave such information as was demanded, or alternatively, the object that was sought. Yet if he gave the object, it wasn't all of it. The murderer has not yet recovered the Milton Cross. . . . Any further ideas on the subject?'

Roberts slowly shook his head. 'Nothing worth examining at close quarters.'

'I think I have. Remember that our first hint of the truth came to us because of the connection between Parlant and Brindle in their legal capacity? We now have another person to include—Blair the prisoner. Where would these three come together except at a consultation?'

'Seems reasonable, sir.'

'That consultation took place in the police cells or prison; it must have done, and it was there that Parlant and Brindle learned about the Milton Cross. We can now go one step further: because they have been unable to provide all the answers to the murderer, there must have been a third man who also shared the secret, received his share of the Cross. . . . That's the man I've got to trace.'

'Bit of a tall order.'

'Is it?'

'Isn't it?'

'By etiquette, silk never moves without a junior, does he?'

'Nor he does,' replied Roberts, his voice rising from excitement.

*

Mr. Tolby was awakened from a dream of much pleasure of the kind which leaves behind no memories bar the vague sense of goodwill once it is over. He stared at the figure by the side of his bed, and all thoughts of goodwill vanished.

'Sorry this should happen again,' said Blackshirt.

Mr. Tolby was also exceedingly sorry, and his anger was increased by the fact that since the other knew he wore a nightgown he need not desist from expressing his feelings because of fear for his taboo. 'What do you want?'

'A little more information.'

'Go away and leave me in peace.'

'I wish I could.'

Mr. Tolby thought the remark so hypocritical it was impossible to reply to it in decent terms.

'Who was old man Parlant's junior in the Blair case?'

'Mr. Ernest Parlant had as junior Mr. Timothy Brenchley,' snapped the clerk.

Beneath his hood Blackshirt grinned. He had thought the reference to "old man Parlant" would produce some reaction. 'Decent type, Brenchley?'

'A barrister has to be a gentleman to be granted the privilege of being called to the Bar,' was the angry retort.

'Did he do much work in the Blair case?'

'Naturally.'

Blackshirt realized that his shaft of attempted humour had back-fired, and that he had, in the eyes of the clerk, committed a very serious solecism. He hastened to try to remedy matters and spoke humbly. 'I'm sorry, but I've never known exactly what it was a junior did.'

Mr. Tolby was shocked that anyone could be so ignorant, but felt the gravity of the situation was slightly ameliorated by the obvious desire of the other to learn. He therefore condescended to explain what part a junior took in a case where silk was briefed, a question many a lay client had asked when called upon to pay the fees of both the two counsel and the solicitor. 'Mr. Brenchley was a very fine junior,' he finally said.

'Was?' queried Blackshirt.

'He died, quite suddenly, poor man. Said good-bye when he left chambers one day in a perfectly normal manner, yet two hours later he was dead.'

'Normally?'

'I beg your pardon?'

'Did he die from normal causes.'

'Of course. Barristers are not in the habit of . . .' Mr. Tolby did not complete what he had been going to say. Barristers were not in the habit of coming to violent ends, but it might be argued that Mr. Justice Parlant had started the fashion.

'Was his death long after the Blair case?'

The clerk tried to remember. 'I suppose it must have been two years.'

'Was Brenchley at the consultation between Blair and Mr. Ernest Parlant?'

'Of course . . .' The Clerk paused, thought. 'I seem to remember something unusual happened. Mr. Brenchley was ill and . . . or did he have to leave hurriedly to do another case? . . . That's it! He and Mr. Ernest Parlant went to the police court for the preliminary hearing, and I had to telephone Mr. Brenchley and ask him to come straight back to chambers.'

'Then he had nothing to do with the case?'

'Later on, yes. It was only that first day he was away.'

'Wasn't it unusual to brief such formidable counsel for the preliminary hearing?'

Mr. Tolby looked undecided. 'If the case is very serious, some clients feel much happier that way.' He stared at the ceiling. 'But there was something very odd about this case, and I can't remember what it was.' Sadly he shook his head. 'One's memory does not last as age creeps on.'

'What kind of oddness?'

'As I've just said, I can't remember.'

Blackshirt hastily tried to soothe the other's feelings, which became ruffled all too easily. 'I wonder if you'd know whether it was to do with the case itself, or with the people concerned? The general, rather than the specific?'

'I have no idea.'

There was a silence. Blackshirt wondered if there were anything more to be gained from interviewing the clerk, grinned wryly. "More" seemed the wrong word to use, when nothing had been learned. . . . Yet that was not correct, either. One fact had been established. The Junior had not been present at the first consultation, but had been at later ones. This left two possibilities. Either it had been one of the later consultations in which the future of the Milton Cross was decided, or else the junior was not the missing man. How he, Blackshirt, was to prove which solution was the correct one, with both men dead, was something he could not foresee.

'Anything more you want to know?' demanded Mr. Tolby.

'Don't think so.'

'Then would it be asking too much of you to leave?'

'I'll do that,' replied Blackshirt. 'If I want any more information,' he added thoughtfully, 'I can always drop in and see you again.'

Although he knew nothing about firearms, and had always regarded them with horror, Mr. Tolby decided it was time he bought a sporting gun and kept it by his bedside, loaded and ready. He was a peaceful man, eschewing violence in any form, yet the one thing which would have brought him joy was the sight of Blackshirt's body shot to ribbons. Even the thought of so delectable an occurrence filled his mind with pleasure.

He watched the cracksman leave the room, sighed as he realized he would be much too scared to pull the trigger. He was about to snuggle down beneath the covers of the bed and seek sleep once more when a thought occurred to him. It was his duty as a good citizen to report what had just taken place. He climbed from the bed, wrapped a dressing-gown tightly about himself, made his way downstairs. He entered the front room, telephoned the police. He was very annoyed when his good-citizenship was so cavalierly treated.

Chapter Seven

VERRELL folded the thickish piece of writing paper, folded it again, twisted part of it back on itself, half turned it inside out. About to congratulate himself, he stopped, looked with annoyance at what should have been a most excellent form of dart but most certainly was not. He tried again, and was in the middle of a revised form of construction when Roberts entered the room carrying a tray.

Roberts placed the tray down on a convenient table, stared at what Verrell had been doing, and allowed his features to express maximum disapproval that he should find his employer not working at his book as was supposed to be the case.

'Stuck for the moment,' explained Verrell.

'Yes, sir. . . . Sugar and milk?'

Verrell wondered why it was that other people always thought authors should work all hours of the day and night. What was the point in being an author unless one sat back and did no work, since it was only because one was what one was, that one could act in such manner? 'Both please,' he said finally in answer to the query.

Roberts poured out the coffee, passed the cup across.

'I've got no further,' said Verrell.

'So I see, sir,' remarked Roberts severely.

'With Mr. Tolby.'

For once, the valet was overcome by the human failing of curiosity, and was forced to ask, 'What happened?'

'The junior, Brenchley, was not present at the first consultation with the accused, but was at the later ones.'

'Does that tell you'nothing?'

'I haven't decided.'

'Whatever took place with regard to the diamonds could have happened at a later meeting, couldn't it?'

'Of course—but instinct tells me no. Blair must have been caught off-balance to give away the whereabouts of the Cross. It seems to me that that could only have happened immediately after he was taken into custody.'

'But if the junior wasn't present, who was?' asked Roberts.

'That's the sixty-four thousand dollar question.'

'What are you going to do now?'

'Try and find out what was the odd happening that Tolby thought had taken place. If it was sufficiently odd, it'll be in the papers of that date.'

Verrell drank the coffee and reflected how the world was sharply divided into those who could make it, and those who could not. Roberts was in the former class; most other people were in the latter.

*

Past numbers of the newspaper were kept in a large basement that had been divided into small spaces by the parallel shelves that ran from end to end. These shelves were filled with the bound newspapers stacked in date order.

There was a strange fascination in reading the news of so many years before. Time and time again, Verrell found his attention distracted away from the search for some reference to the arrest of Albert Blair, to some item that had nothing to do with that gentleman. Most interesting of all were the prognostications about the future of all subjects made by experts who obviously knew what they were talking about. The years had dealt harshly with their mirror-gazing, and in some cases themselves.

Verrell took down a second volume, replaced the first. Rapidly, he checked through the pages, rigorously denying himself the pleasure of roaming. He completed the search of that volume, exchanged it for another.

By now there was an empty feeling within him that suggested it must be time to eat, and a quick glance at his watch confirmed his inner alarum-clock. He sighed, looked at the date of the newspaper he was searching. It was a much later day than that on which Blair had been arrested. Either he had missed such reference as there had been, or there was none.

He left the building, had lunch at a nearby restaurant that charged a great deal of money for a very poor meal, returned to the newspaper office, turned back and began the search once more.

By now, the fascination of the search had gone, and the task was merely laborious. Verrell checked each headline, and if there were any possibility that the subject matter might concern Albert Blair, read quickly through the descriptive passage beneath.

He found what he sought under a heading he all but ignored for the second time. The headline read: "Clergyman unconscious in cell." The paragraph was brief and described how a clergyman, taken into custody the night before, had fallen unconscious while in consultation with his lawyers. He had been attended by a doctor and the cause for his illness was found to be nothing serious. At the conclusion of this report was a short sentence to the effect that Mr. Ernest Parlant, Q.C., was counsel.

Verrell read the report three times, turned to the next day's paper. Nothing more was reported, nor did he find any further reference to the case. Without any reluctance on his part he decided nothing more was to be gained by further search, and after he had replaced the volumes on the shelf, left the building.

He walked slowly, threading his way along the crowded pavement automatically and without conscious care. He thought about his next move, wondered what it should be, when it should take place.

*

The town was representative of so many others. Once possessing charm, it now possessed instead multiple stores which seemed to vie with one another as to which could provide the most aesthetically objectionable frontage. The roads could not support the traffic that used them, and a by-pass, having been under discussion for a mere ten years, was hardly within the realms of possibility.

The Magistrates' Court was in the main police station, an ugly red-bricked building halfway along one of the side roads. The court was ill-lit, ill-ventilated, and had on the Bench one retired admiral, two colonels, one butcher, and two ardent feminists, all of whom were dogged by the necessity to administer justice, but none of whom knew the meaning of the word. They placed great reliance on their clerk, a solicitor who was exceedingly friendly with the Inspector of the local police. The percentage of convictions being thus extremely high, it was fondly believed that law and order reigned, and the only time there was any sense of trouble was when a prisoner demanded his right to be tried by a higher court.

Verrell sat at the back of the court and watched. The Justices stared ahead of themselves with expressions of gravity and decorum. The witness in the box looked bored, the three policemen present looked bored, the lawyers looked even more bored, and the other two members of the public were probably asleep. Only the prisoner seemed to find anything of interest in the proceedings.

The case continued on its weary way and all evidence was laboriously taken down in longhand, any more modern means of reproduction being apparently unknown.

At twelve-thirty the Court was adjourned, and the Justices, amidst much pomp and ceremony, departed from their court. A suggestion of life returned to those who remained.

Verrell stood up and was glad to do so, the wooden benches allowed the public being notoriously uncomfortable. He watched a man in civilian clothes speak to two of the uniformed constables. On one of their faces there appeared a broad grin that rapidly vanished as he was addressed in an unfriendly manner.

Verrell left the courtroom, made his way to the door which led out to the street. Immediately opposite the police station was a public house: this was the kind of omen only a madman would ignore. Verrell was perfectly sane.

'Pint of bitter,' he ordered.

'Hot weather, sir—good for the crops.'

'And for drinking?'

The bartender smiled. 'Heat brings them in to cool off; cold brings them in to warm-up; wet brings them in to dry-off; dry brings them in to wet-up.' He turned, picked up a glass mug, filled it with two steady pulls on the pump handle. He set the glass before Verrell.

The beer was good and formed an excellent anodyne to the warmth of the day. As Verrell drank, he pondered the problem of how he was to do that which he had come to the town to do. Where would he find someone who would remember the clergyman who had fainted, would be able to fill in the outline the newspaper had so roughly sketched?

'Bless my soul!' announced the bartender suddenly.

Verrell noticed the look of astonishment on the other's face, turned. A constable in uniform entered, came up to the bar. 'Half of mild, Joe.'

'What's up with you coming in here like this—looking for your pension?'

The constable winked. 'Come in to ask a few questions.' He put a two-shilling piece on the glass-topped counter.

'What if old Crusty comes in for a quick one?'

'Always goes to the Grapes.'

'He would.' The bartender drew the half-pint, laid the glass before the constable. 'Busy?'

'Always will be with blokes like you still loose.'

They both laughed. The constable turned, looked about himself. He nodded at Verrell, the only other person present. 'Nice kind of a day for a drink.'

'Couldn't be better,' agreed Verrell.

'Down from London?'

'Don't I look like a local citizen?'

The constable finished what was in his glass in one mighty gulp. 'Wouldn't have said you was from about here, myself, but one can't tell. These days we get a lot of London people who live down here and go up each morning. That's right, isn't it, Joe?'

The bartender agreed that it was so.

The constable regarded his empty glass with such disfavour Verrell had not the heart not to call for the refill.

'Cheers!' said the constable. He brought the glass up to his lips, drank, sighed with satsifaction.

'Been here a long time?' asked Verrell.

'Tidy long time. All my life not two miles from here, and been wearing the blue for over fifteen years.'

'Have you always been attached to this division?'

'Without a break. . . . Thanks, sir.' He accepted the cigarette and the light. 'Life's no worse than most, and there's a nice pension at the end of things. . . . Interesting, too. See some funny things we do, even in a smallish town like this.'

Verrell's face showed no change of expression, yet within him was a sudden quickening of interest. It was to uncover a "funny thing" that he had come to the town. 'Such as?'

The constable lowered the contents of the glass tankard by half before he answered. 'All sorts, that's what we get here. A little bit of everything, and a lot of some things. Some of the cases we've had, you wouldn't believe me if I told you about them.'

'Is that so?'

The bartender rested his elbows on the counter. 'There's not one word of a lie there. . . . Tell him about the man that was so certain he was a monkey.'

The constable related the story so proficiently, and all the ends were so neatly tied up, it was clear it had been repeated many times previously.

Verrell laughed where the story called for laughter, expressed astonishment when that was in order. He finished his drink, called for another round, this time to include the bartender.

'Then there was the time we was on the look-out for an escaped prisoner and I saw an old woman walking down the street.' The constable paused, drank deeply, continued with his story.

Verrell lit a cigarette. Very soon he could introduce one or two questions of his own—the chance of "pumping" a man as loquacious as the one before him was not to be missed.

'Mustn't forget the parson what passed out, either.'

Because he had been about to introduce the name of Blair it came as a shock to Verrell to hear the case referred to without any prompting on his part. The sense of shock passed almost immediately; a feeling of disquietude did not.

Anyone who relied often on instinctive reaction learned to trust it even when apparently in flat contradiction with logic. There was absolutely no reason why Verrell should find cause for uneasiness in the fact that the constable had mentioned the Blair case; after all, Verrell himself had been about to introduce it. Yet somewhere within him there sounded a warning bell.

Without appearing to do so, he studied the constable, and it seemed to him there was a certain tenseness about the other. He tried to discover whether this were really so, or whether he judged it to be thus because of his own sudden feelings. He needed time in which to think, and took his cigarette case from his pocket, offered it around. As he passed it to the constable he looked beyond the latter's shoulder. He could see the road, and standing there was another constable. It could be coincidence; it could be something else.

'. . . And there we found a bloke all dressed up in parson's clothes—brought him into the station and locked him up for the night.'

Verrell knew that it might well be considered madness to close the flood-gates just as they had opened exactly as he had wished, yet he was determined to do so, even should he spend the next few days informing himself of what an idiot he had been.

He looked at his watch, started. 'Hell's bells!' he said, 'I'm supposed to be meeting someone five minutes ago.' He lifted up his glass, drained it.

'You've got to be going?' asked the constable.

He smiled. 'If I don't, I'll collect a real packet. Thanks for the stories, sorry I haven't time to hear the rest of them.' He crossed to the door, opened it, stepped out on to the pavement. The constable who had been outside was no longer in sight.

He walked along the pavement. Had he been an idiot? Had he seen danger where none existed? Instinct could go awry since it depended so much on the mental state of the person at that moment.

The police knew Blackshirt had asked Mr. Tolby about the Blair case. They knew he must be continuing the search, at the end of which was the Milton Cross. It would have needed little perspicacity on their part to work out that his next move must be to try and trace who it was had been present at the consultation with Blair, and that to do that recourse would probably be had to the police in the town to try to discover if there were anyone left who remembered what had happened. Having determined that, they could so easily have gone one step further and decided they had been presented with a wonderful opportunity of catching Blackshirt. He would visit the town and would be interested in Blair. What better way of trapping the cracksman than that of sending out constables to drink and talk freely, targets for someone who wanted information?

Had he allowed the police too much imaginative thinking, or had he avoided a well-baited trap? It might be impossible ever to say.

What was his next move? He pondered the problem, came to a conclusion. If the police had been alerted, they would have studied their own records, started an investigation. Such records would be kept handy for easy reference. . . . They said there was always more than one way of killing a cat.

*

Night inevitably seemed to find the town unprepared. The street lighting was old and ugly, and lamp standards of confused ironwork held lamps that seemed to be perpetually shrouded in mist. Roads were large areas of dark split apart by the dim light. Few buildings showed life, and none of the shops did. The town went to sleep early, and only the heretic or the foreigner stayed awake.

This state of deserted streets helped, yet hindered, Blackshirt. The fear of being overlooked at the moment of entry could be discounted, but the sight of a pedestrian after a certain hour was probably enough to waken suspicion in any constable. It was for this reason that he took a car from the far end of the town, drove back towards the police station, and parked less than twenty yards from it in a space that was already occupied by two other cars.

To say that to break into a police station was the limit of foolhardiness was to state the obvious with such force the words would have well become a politician. Yet this was not completely correct—or so Blackshirt assured himself. The obvious always carried within itself a hint of weakness, merely because it was the obvious. No one would ever be fool enough to try to break into a police station; hence there was no need to guard against such happening.

He had, by careful study, made out the plan of the building in which were the police station and the courtroom. He knew which was the Inspector's room and how that could best be approached. If he found nothing there, he could search the next room, which was used by two sergeants. If that also failed, then he must retire. The risk became too great even for him to contemplate.

He grinned.

He left the car, crossed to within the shadows of a high wall, adjusted gloves and hood.

He felt an unusual prickling of excitement within him. He was not surprised, and as he moved forward towards the window of the Inspector's room, he told himself he ought to be safely locked away in a place where they cared for people who acted as insanely as was he. He chuckled. The police would support that motion.

He stood in the small alleyway that led from the road to the rather tattered churchyard, and listened. He heard nothing beyond the normal night noises.

He took from his belt of tools a short strip of metal that was thin but tough. Eased between the two halves of the window, it came hard up against the catch that secured one to the other. Gradually, he forced the catch back.

He paused. For a brief moment his mind insisted on detailing once again the chances he was taking by breaking into a police station, but he cut short such dismal thoughts. He was a cracksman because he enjoyed, and needed, the excitement. He should not then complain, when he found more of that precious commodity than usual.

He lifted the lower half of the window so slowly it took him an age to complete the operation. He waited, listened to the sounds that now came to him from inside the building, and could make out nothing to alarm.

He drew himself up on to the window-sill, climbed over it into the room. He took his torch from the belt, shone it about him.

The room was poorly furnished, containing nothing beyond two desks, two filing cabinets, two chairs that were usable and two that were not, one hat-stand, a waste-paper basket, a pin-up calendar, and a set of four lithographs of such repellent nature Blackshirt was tempted to remove them for the good of the community.

He crossed to the first desk, on the top of which was a litter of papers, checked through them and found cinema ticket stubs, torn-up bookmaker's tickets and a theatre programme. He found nothing such as he sought. He checked through the drawers of the desk and was relieved when they proved to be in comparative order. Again he discovered nothing.

He crossed to the second desk. The papers here were tidied to geometric precision. The pencils were parallel to the ruler, the ruler was at right angles to the blotting-paper which was precisely in the centre of the desk, and on top of which the two folders had been most carefully squared.

He opened the first folder. It contained one half-page of typing, and this reported on a theft that had taken place the previous day and the culprit of which had been apprehended within two hours of the crime. Blackshirt checked the second folder. Inside were records of Edward Johnson, one-time constable in the police force.

He read through the papers, closed the folder, replaced it most precisely in position.

Why was Constable Johnson the subject of an investigation? The reports were all dated, and had been drawn up within the last day or two, yet the constable had retired from the police force several years previously when the legacy from an aunt had provided him with sufficient money to retire. Blackshirt checked the date of the retirement. It was within six months of Blair's arrest.

It was inevitable that he should wish to believe he had found what he sought. The quoted dates matched sufficiently well the dates he was checking. A police constable could have, so reasonably, been at the consultation. The aunt's legacy could so easily be the value of the Milton Cross.

Although he, logically, propounded questions to himself, and then answered them, there was never any doubt as to what he would do. Blackshirt had never been known for lack of curiosity.

*

The constable had moved to a village fifty miles away. Verrell drove those fifty miles in little over the hour, along roads that most would have said were incapable of offering such speed. But then, most people had never driven with Verrell, which was as well, especially for the fainthearted.

He stopped the car by the side of the road and searched for the map in the glove compartment beneath the dashboard. After a quick check he became certain he was within two miles of his destination as the proverbial crow flew, three and a half as the country lane went.

During the journey he had considered all he knew, had allowed himself certain reasonable surmises, and had reached certain conclusions.

The police had searched their own records, and for reasons at which he could only guess had decided that the retired Constable Johnson could stand some investigating. Having said this, they then went one stage further and reckoned that whoever was of interest to them, would undoubtedly also be of interest to Blackshirt, who, they knew, was working along the same lines as were they. At this point one thing became clear—a unique opportunity was afforded them to know what were Blackshirt's future plans.

The cracksman wondered if he were being altogether too fanciful? Would the police have thought as he estimated they would? Surely the man who sat behind the neat desk would never have followed so many untidy twists and turns of thought? . . . But the man who sat at the untidy desk might have done! And how was he to know whether the ideas had not come from further afield—from Superintendent Ashley, for instance.

Fanciful or not, he knew he must be even more careful than he normally was.

He backed the car into the lane behind him and stopped the engine. There was a long, and probably arduous, walk ahead of him, but if he drove nearer to the house the noise of his approach, followed by the sudden cessation of the engine, would warn the watchers.

He crossed several fields, reached the junction of two blackthorn hedges and knew he was at the end of the triangular field which lay to the rear of the house.

Somewhere in the right-hand hedge he expected to find a gate, and when he was half-way along he reached it.

He felt the gate with his hands, noted that it was a normal wooden one. He remembered the time he had blundered into a trap because a gate had been wired to an alarm, and checked all about the support posts but found nothing. Still not satisfied, he felt immediately above the gate, and his hand came in contact with a fine thread.

He opened the gate, crawled underneath the thread, crossed the small stretch of field with as much care as if it had been a mine-field came to another gate that was sufficiently near the house that he could make out its black bulk against the starry sky. This second gate was free of any form of alarm.

He wondered where the watchers were, decided they must be some little way away from the house. Satisfied, he then characteristically forgot them, concentrated entirely on entering the house. He walked over the lawn, came to a brick path and crossed this in complete silence. He checked on the lock of the back door, took a small strip of mica from his pocket, forced open the lock, entered the house.

In the bedroom that was lined with genuine oak panelling Johnson snored happily, revelling in the freedom of one who lived alone and could thus afford to enjoy such luxuries.

He felt the hand shake his shoulder, and the terror of the sudden awakening seemed to crush deep down in his chest.

A pin-prick of light came into being and played over his face.

'Don't get excited,' said a voice.

The advice, given in a voice of amused tolerance, made Johnson more nervous than ever, and were it not for a feeling of certainty that such action would be of no more use than it had been in childhood, he would have plunged beneath the bed-clothes to escape the goblins and warlocks.

'Who . . .?' His voice refused to continue.

'Blackshirt.'

He gasped, and his face expressed terror. 'What do you want?' he whispered.

'Information.'

'Why d'you come here?'

'The result of natural consequences.'

'You can't kill me.' Johnson's voice was shrill. He suddenly shifted sideways, an action that increased by six inches the distance between himself and the intruder.

'I've no intention of doing so,' snapped Blackshirt.

'You killed those other two.'

'That's a damned lie.' The accusation filled him with anger.

'You killed them.'

He came nearer to the frightened man on the bed. 'I killed neither man: I'm here to find out who did.'

'The papers . . .'

'The newspapers don't always print the truth. I have never committed murder in the past, nor shall I ever do so.'

Johnson slowly relaxed. The terror left his eyes, his lips closed so that his teeth were no longer visible, and he shifted his body until it lay at a more natural position. 'What was the information?' He spoke in a voice that still quavered slightly, but the harsh whistle of fear was gone.

'Remember the Milton Cross, Johnson?'

'Kind of.'

'Where is it?'

'Got stolen, didn't it?' Johnson's facial expression changed from one of fear to one of extreme wariness.

'You should know.'

'Why me?'

'You stole it.'

'What the hell are you talking about?'

Blackshirt spoke coldly. 'Cut out the clowning, Johnson. You stole the Milton Cross from Albert Blair, sold it, or part of it, within six months of the theft, used the money to enable you to retire from the police force, come here, and buy this house.'

'My aunt left me the money.'

'That's for the records—I want the facts.'

'You reckon?'

'I reckon.'

'You're full of bright ideas,' sneered Johnson. It was amazing how quickly he changed from coward to brave man.

'Do I get the story?'

'You don't get nothing from me because I ain't got nothing to give.'

'You haven't stopped to think that a little co-operation might save yourself a whole pile of trouble?'

'I tell you I ain't got nothing to co-operate about.'

Blackshirt realized he had made a bad tactical error. Had he let the other continue to believe him a murderer, he would, by now, have learned all he wished to know. But he had been too eager to defend his reputation, had momentarily forgotten the job in hand, and as a result had lost the initiative.

He moved slowly, sat down on the edge of the bed and allowed the torch to lie in such a way that the light from it outlined himself.

There was silence.

Johnson lost much of his hastily acquired courage, began to fidget, to arrange and rearrange the bedclothes about his chin. His eyelids blinked more and more rapidly.

'What did you tell the police?' asked Blackshirt quietly.

'What police?'

'The ones who, in the past few days, have asked you numerous questions about the Blair case?'

'No one's asked anything.'

'No?' Blackshirt paused for a few seconds to gain the maximum effect from timing. 'Then why have they got, in a distant police station, a folder concerning you and all your details?'

Again Johnson experienced fear, but this time, because the danger was remote, in distance if not potency, his mind was not filled by it to the extent of panicking. 'You're spouting nonsense.'

'D'you think I troubled to come all the way here to do that?'

Johnson tried not to ask the question, but the desire to do so was not to be denied. 'What's in the folder?'

'Your particulars, newly brought up to date. . . . They're investigating, amongst other things, the death of your aunt—that most fortunate occurrence for you.'

'She died.'

'Did she fall, or was she pushed?'

Johnson ignored the facetious question. He stared at the cracksman, looked hurriedly away. He tried to speak twice, succeeded only in pronouncing the first sound of the first word. He licked his lips, waited until he had more control, then said, 'They've got nothing on me.'

'Only the Milton Cross.'

'I don't know nothing about it.'

'I don't believe that—nor do the police.'

He looked in the direction of the door as though he expected it suddenly to open and admit a storm of policemen. 'That folder don't prove anything.'

'Your repeated denials might persuade me—if it weren't for one other thing.'

Again, he had to ask: 'What's that?'

Blackshirt spoke very calmly. 'This house is being watched by the police.'

Johnson swallowed heavily and his face contorted. 'That's a lie.'

'Why should I lie about such a matter?'

'To frighten me.'

'Is that logical, considering I had you so frightened when I first arrived you all but took off to the nearest grave?'

Johnson pulled the sheet away from him, ran his hand round his neck. Small beads of sweat on his forehead glistened in the light. 'Where are they?'

'Within striking distance of the front door.'

'What do they want?'

Blackshirt sighed. 'You seem to like every 't' crossed and every 'i' dotted, three times. They want the Milton Cross.'

'They won't find anything here.'

'Don't expect they will.'

'I've never seen it.'

'You were around when Blair was taken into custody, weren't you?'

'That doesn't mean a thing.'

'Neither I nor the police agree with you—nor does the other man.'

'What . . . What other man?'

'The killer. He found Parlant and Brindle; won't be long before he finds you.'

Johnson quite suddenly showed a form of courage that was as surprising as it was unexpected. 'He's got no cause to come after me—but if he does, I know how to look after myself.'

The ex-police constable was a complex mixture of courage and cowardice. Perhaps, thought Blackshirt, he could face the abstract with equanimity, but was overwhelmed by reality, in direct contrast to many.

'Parlant and Brindle probably thought the same way as you do,' said the cracksman.

'What the hell does it matter what they thought?'

'If you can think straight, ponder this. If I get the Cross first, the killer will have to give up. That way you'd have a chance to continue living.'

'You're not so flaming clever, Mr. Blackshirt. I never saw the Cross, don't know where it went to or where it is now.'

The cracksman studied Johnson, came to the conclusion that if he were lying there was no way at the moment of proving it, or of making him tell the truth. Blackshirt stood up, moved away from the bed.

'Going?' asked Johnson sneeringly.

'For the moment.'

'Don't bother to call back.'

'I'll be seeing you again,' promised Blackshirt, 'and next time you'll be talking.'

Johnson watched the cracksman walk away, merge into the black of the distant parts of the room, and vanish.

*

It was sometimes said that Blackshirt's sense of humour had never grown beyond adolescence. This was a gross over-exaggeration, but it was true that quite often his actions did seem to be dictated by a rather carefree and gay abandonment. Such was the time when he approached, in complete silence, to within three feet of the two men who were watching Johnson's house, and then shouted the loudest "Boo" of which he was capable.

Chapter Eight

INSPECTOR CHARING, of the Greencliffe police, stared at Detective Constables Seeton and Dean. It was a look of great feeling, none of which was pleasant.

The constables studied their boots and the floor.

'I hope,' remarked the Inspector, 'he didn't frighten you too, too much?'

They remained silent, unwilling to admit, even to themselves, what had happened. They had both been smoking, against orders, and had, therefore, kept the cigarettes well hidden. As the sound, which at the time they incorrectly identified as the last trump, rent the air, shock had all but stretched them out, bloodless corpses. In the excitement Seeton dropped his cigarette inside his shirt; Dean let his fall into the right-hand turn-up of his trousers. Seeton, before he had recovered from the shock, suddenly entered into a frenzied dance, at the same time performing an impromptu strip-tease. Dean, amused, despite all that had recently passed, had been laughing immoderately when he found other causes to consider. His trousers were on fire. No man is at his best when that happens.

'Perhaps you ought to see the doctor and have a thorough check. You're far too valuable to the police force for us to take any chances.'

The constables consoled themselves with the knowledge that the Inspector was a pompous idiot at the best of times.

'Didn't you chide Blackshirt for his inconsiderateness?'

They found their boots even more interesting.

'Haven't you anything to say?'

Dean coughed. 'The alarm didn't go off, sir.'

'Dear me, how annoying! I must speak to the makers and point out in the strongest terms that when my men go on duty they ought to be able to go to sleep knowing they can rely on the alarm waking them before trouble starts.'

'We didn't sleep,' protested Dean.

'No?' The Inspector forgot his resolution that he would contain his temper, slammed clenched fist down on the top of the desk and began to shout. 'You were both asleep on duty. Without a shadow of doubt. . . .'

There was a knock at the door, which then opened. A constable entered. 'Superintendent Ashley and Detective-Sergeant Hooper, sir.'

The two men from London walked in. They shook hands with the Inspector.

'I hope,' said Ashley, 'everything is all right now?'

Dean and Seeton, despite their natural antipathy towards anyone called in from London to give a hand, felt warmly towards Ashley as they noted how the Inspector received those few words; nor was their pleasure dimmed by the knowledge that their turn would almost certainly come.

The Inspector was thought to mumble something.

'Pity Blackshirt got away,' continued the Superintendent, 'but then these things will happen.' He smiled. It was the kind of smile an executioner used when he tested, and found to his liking, the edge of his axe.

'He . . . that is . . . I mean . . .'

'Yes?'

The Inspector remained silent.

Ashley was at a disadvantage, since these men were not under his command and he could not, therefore, tell them precisely what he thought. However, by the use of somewhat over-enthusiastic sarcasm he managed to let them know how they would have been treated had they worked for him.

The constables were finally allowed to go, the Inspector was asked if his room might be borrowed. Only too thankfully he agreed, left them.

'What a lovely shower,' said Hooper rudely.

'Must you be so polite?'

'I reckon they've escaped from the nearest mortuary.'

Ashley groaned. 'They knew he was coming to that house. They knew it, yet look what happened! It's enough to make a man weep!'

'Wish I'd been around,' said Hooper.

'That would have been a lot of good,' sneered the Superintendent. 'Remember what happened last time you came face to face with Blackshirt?'

Hooper remembered. The Detective-Sergeant consigned his superior to a far-away place, then remembered that Ashley, himself, had not shown up so well in that encounter.

'What now?' asked Ashley, a few moments later.

'I reckon a word or two with Johnson wouldn't be a waste of time.'

He took a cigarette from a battered packet, affixed it to his lip, lit it. 'Might as well try to salvage something from the wreckage. . . . To think they knew he was coming, Bill.' He found it difficult, still, to accept the facts.

They were driven to Johnson's house, and there they met the owner, were shown into the sitting-room, and offered drinks. These they accepted at once.

'Nice set-up you've got here,' remarked Ashley appreciatively.

Johnson nodded his head.

'Bit of a difference to the old days?'

'Yes.' Only at the last moment did he prevent himself adding, 'sir.'

'Fortunate you had an aunt like you did.'

'She always liked me.'

'Understandable,' said Ashley. The police had investigated the death of the aunt, had checked and double-checked the will, and regrettably found it was perfectly true that she had left him all she possessed. People had been astonished by the large sum of money, in one-pound notes, that had been found hidden in one of the many trunks in her attic, but astonishment was all that had been expressed, and the money had eventually, after the lawyers had been forced to withdraw their sticky talons, passed down to Johnson. Ashley was certain how that money had come to be in the trunk, but could find no way in which to set about proving it.

'I used to look after her,' said Johnson, in tones of voice that declared he had dedicated himself to her welfare.

'Why didn't you report that Blackshirt had visited you last night?' snapped the Superintendent suddenly.

'I was going to. . . .'

'Stuff and nonsense. When the Inspector came here and interviewed you, because of what two of his men had reported, you had had several hours in which to make a report but had done nothing about it.'

'I told the Inspector——'

'A pack of lies.'

Johnson plucked up his courage. 'You seem to know more about the matter than I do,' he replied belligerently.

'Why didn't you make a report?'

'Who says I've got to? Tell me that one! I don't know of no law that says I've got to tell the police if someone breaks into my house. Do you?'

The Superintendent did not.

'Then everything's fine.'

'Any honest man would have. . . .'

'Are you saying I'm not honest?' demanded Johnson.

Ashley swallowed hard, and reminded himself that a crook was only a crook when so proved. 'Of course not,' he said reluctantly, hoping that soon he would gain proof that Johnson had been guilty of every crime in the statute books.

'That's a good job, isn't it? Might have had to speak severely to you.' He laughed. 'Care for another drink just before you go?'

'No, thanks.'

'Sorry I couldn't be of more help to you.'

The police left the house. They climbed into the car and were driven away. 'To think Blackshirt didn't even black an eye for him,' groaned Ashley.

*

Johnson had to be made to talk. How? Verrell paced up and down the room, trying to find a solution to the problem.

He reached the far end of the room and was within striking distance of the cocktail cabinet. The hint was too obvious to be missed, and he busied himself mixing a John Collins.

He sipped his drink and noted with approval that the various proportions were exactly right. He lit a cigarette, blew two smoke rings towards the ceiling, then a third that was supposed to race the first two, but which, in fact, disintegrated immediately.

He sat down in the nearest armchair, leaned back, and allowed his mind to wander at will from subject to subject, as he would do when his writing would not proceed; and in the same undefinable and wholly mysterious way that his characters would decide their future actions, so quite suddenly, he had the solution.

He grinned. He thought it likely Johnson would regard his next move in the light of a dirty trick. He stood up, crossed to the cocktail cabinet, mixed himself another drink. Genius deserved a reward.

*

The district was good hunting country, and although within moderately easy reach of London was beyond the immediate expansion of that amorphous mass and was well populated by big houses. Some of these had inevitably been taken over on behalf of the bureaucrats who plundered the country, but the majority still housed private families.

89

The first house Blackshirt visited was built in the shape of the letter E, and would have been extremely attractive had not some previous owner caused to be built a pillared entrance with circular steps and several stone cherubs and other winged beings whose attractiveness was in no way increased by the fact that they all had suffered some form of damage. What had been a well-proportioned house of much elegance became a stockbroker's warty mansion.

Blackshirt, thankfully unconcerned with aesthetic values, chose one of the side doors, and after forty-nine seconds' work, entered the house. As soon as a careful check had made certain that all was quiet, he chose to start work in the study where there was a safe that could not have been much less old than the house. This he opened with ease. Inside was the family silver and also several pieces of jewellery, none of which was very valuable. Blackshirt chose three pieces of silver and two of the diamond rings. He then left the room, having made certain the safe door was open, and returned downstairs.

The second house he visited had been built for a business man who had had the sense to go bankrupt twice, early in his career, and had thus amassed a considerable fortune by the time he was forty. His tastes were not always of the best, and nothing the architect could say would change his ideas on what he wanted. Among the villagers the house was known as the midden.

The businessman was inclined to be cautious, and the house was in his wife's name, the three cars were run by his firms, and his pigs died at regular intervals, so making certain that the farm was run at a loss year after year. He had but one vanity, and that was himself, and no trouble was too great to make certain he was always immaculately dressed. He wore gold collar studs, platinum cuff-links, pearl buttons on his waistcoats, and diamond tie-pins. Blackshirt chose the best of the studs, cuff-links, buttons, and tie-pins, then left.

The last house he entered was of solid, no-nonsense, English style. It was hot in the summer, cold in the winter, the windows faced north, and the fireplaces smoked. The present owner was M.F.H. three days a week, and on the other four president of the local society that campaigned against cruelty to animals.

Death duties had left the present owner in reduced circumstances, and such wealth as remained would soon be lost because he was a basically honest man.

Blackshirt found a small silver cup which had been presented to the owner for his invaluable services to the Hunt over the many years. This he took, reckoning to return it as soon as possible, certain its loss would cause more trouble than if he had helped himself to a five-thousand-pound pearl necklace.

Blackshirt drove back to London. He felt pleasantly tired and was conscious of the knowledge of a good job done. He wished he could be a fly, to observe at first hand the reactions of the three people he had visited.

*

Inspector Charing placed the receiver back on its pedestal and there was a strange look on his face.

'What's up?' asked the Sergeant.

'That was old man Gilbert.'

'What's that old basket want?'

'Someone's swiped the cup the Hunt presented him with a couple of years back.'

'No!' ejaculated the Sergeant, an expression of delighted horror on his face. 'Bet he had a few things to say.'

'First time I've come across half the words.'

'Wouldn't I just have loved to see him when he found out.'

The telephone rang again. The Inspector answered it, spoke shortly, listened for a long time, finally replaced the receiver. He sighed. 'That was the Manor. Burglary up there last night.'

'Another? Much gone?'

'Enough.' The Inspector drummed the top of his desk with his fingers. 'Two burglaries the same night. One's rare enough in this part of the world, but two . . .'

Within a short while the score was three.

'What's it add up to?' asked the Sergeant.

'You tell me.'

'Probably nothing more than someone doing a good night's work in one district before moving on to another.'

The Inspector hesitated before answering. 'That's the sensible answer, isn't it? But I don't like it, George. Sometimes I've an instinct for these things.'

'Blowed if I can see anything special to worry about.'

'Nor I—blast it!' He stood up abruptly. 'Can't stay here all day. Let's get cracking, George.'

'Both of us?'

'Most certainly. You can go along and have a word with old Gilbert while I see the others.'

The Sergeant muttered something that was inaudible.

*

Blackshirt reached the gate outside Johnson's house above which had been the thread connected to the alarm. He checked, found it still there, wondered whether it had been left because no one could be sufficiently troubled to remove it, or whether a guard was still being kept. He opened the gate, moved forward underneath the thread.

He reached the house, unlocked the back door, entered, made his way up to Johnson's room. He shook the sleeping man into wakefulness.

Johnson quickly recovered from the initial fright. 'Why the hell do you want coming back here?' he truculently demanded.

'Another little intimate talk.'

'Clear out and leave me alone. Having the police around is bad enough, without tripping over you every time I move my feet.'

Blackshirt ignored the inhospitable welcome, sat down on the bed. He studied Johnson, rapidly came to the conclusion he had never before in the same man found such a combination of bravado and cowardice. 'Have you read the papers lately?' he asked.

Johnson hurried to speak, suddenly hesitated, uncertain, suspicious. 'Why?'

'This district has been in the news.'

'Has it?'

'Especially in the local paper which came out today.'

'So what?'

'Police must have got quite a rocket from those three men who suffered the burglaries—especially where the M.F.H. was concerned.'

'Maybe.' Johnson was rapidly becoming afraid. He knew the words Blackshirt spoke must have special significance, but he could not, as yet, make out what that significance could be.

'When they catch the gentleman concerned they'll lash into him because of the nuisance he's caused them.'

'What's all this got to do with me?'

Blackshirt spoke quite casually. 'You're the man they're looking for.'

'Me?'

'In one.'

'You're crazy. I didn't have a thing to do with those burglaries. I've never broken into a house in my life.'

'I'm afraid that's rather beside the point. They're after you, not because you committed the burglaries, but because they've been led to think that you did.'

Sweat formed on Johnson's forehead and the nervous tic in his eyelid had begun. 'Why should they think that? I haven't done anything.'

'But I have.'

They were silent. Blackshirt stared calmly at the man in the bed; the latter endeavoured to return the gaze, but however much he tried, could not but turn his head away.

Johnson began to speak rapidly, and his voice was shrill. 'What the hell have you been up to? They won't believe anything you say.'

'You should know that facts are indisputable. Witnesses may lie, facts cannot. Stolen property is stolen property, and when found hidden in your house nothing will alter its damning characteristic, nor, because facts are facts, prevent your being named as the man who stole it. The police haven't any great love of you at the moment; they won't be reluctant to remove you to a less salubrious dwelling place.'

'I'll tell them the truth. I'll——'

Blackshirt shook his head. 'No good. Stolen property found hidden about your house, dust from these other places, mud from their gardens. The gloves you wore, missing; the thread found caught in the safe, will be uncovered. Everything necessary for the prosecution to ensure a conviction. . . . And to clamp down any futile hopes, none of these incriminating items is in the house as yet, nor will it be planted until I think it's time. Put quite simply, you'll never know when to search to try and uncover all these things, consequently no search can be effective.' He crossed his hands one over the other, and there was something symbolic about the gesture. 'If I were you, I'd keep a few necessary items packed and ready,' he said dispassionately.

Johnson seemed to have difficulty in understanding all that had been said, but it gradually became clear that that difficulty existed because his mind did not wish to understand, rather than that it could not.

'I'm still open to trading, Johnson. The true story of the Milton Cross might make me change my plans.'

'I . . . I can't.'

'I'd be sorry to see you go to prison, but that seems to be where you're determined to send yourself.'

'It's you, you filthy swine, who's sending me there.'

'Let's cut out the name calling,' suggested Blackshirt softly. He knew he had manoeuvred the other into an untenable position, but it had had to be done. Johnson held the key to the problem, the solution of which had to be gained before Blackshirt could stand before the world untainted by the word "murderer."

The long silence was concluded when Johnson asked hoarsely, 'If I tell you?'

'I'll send the stolen property back to the rightful owners.'

'That's what you say.'

'You'll find my word slightly more trustworthy than most.'

He had, in effect, been left without a choice. He groaned. 'How much do you want to know?'

'Start at the beginning and end at the end.'

Johnson began to speak, and so toneless was his voice it was as though he were a zombie, a description that held good until one noticed the expression in his eyes. They expressed murderous hate. 'I was on duty in the cells to which Blair was brought. The morning after he was caught, two barristers and a solicitor came down to the cells—there wasn't anywhere else for them to see him—to have their conference with him. One of the barristers got called away at once, and it wasn't long before the other left the cell—heard him say he'd go and prepare the brief. No sooner had he gone than Blair's brother came up and asked to see the prisoner.' He stopped speaking, looked across the room at a small cupboard.

'Drink?'

He nodded his head.

Blackshirt crossed to the cupboard and opened it, took out a half-filled bottle of whisky which he carried, together with a glass, to Johnson.

Johnson helped himself to a drink of great size, then continued speaking. ''Course, the brother wasn't supposed to see him right then, but since I was only human . . .'

'A fiver?'

The quick flush that spread over his face showed that the suggestion had not been too wide of the mark. 'I told the brother I'd have to stay with him, and he said that was all right. I took him into the cell just as the solicitor was about to leave. The brother had one look at Blair, dressed in priest's clothes, and roared with laughter. Blair slugged him one, the brother got mad, hit back and laid Blair out. As he fell to the ground the cross around his neck, which had been plain black, hit something and came apart and there was a cross of diamonds. We knew it was the Milton Cross.'

Blackshirt felt a sense of admiration for the dead Blair, despite the fact that the taking of the Milton Cross had been accompanied by such brutal violence. Having stolen the Cross, Blair was fully aware how intensive would be the search for it, and how difficult to sell it immediately. He had chosen to hide it in the most secure of ways: had left it in full view of all.

Johnson continued to speak. 'We stared at the Cross. The huge diamond in the centre reflected the light up to the cell roof like a blazing comet. I kept thinking that just that one big diamond was said to be worth tens of thousands of pounds. I could work all my life and then not make enough even to buy its reflection.'

'Who was the first to suggest taking the Cross?'

'Brindle, the solicitor. He seemed to go mad. He suddenly bent down and picked up the Cross, started caressing the diamonds with his hands. He looked at us, then asked me what I suggested we ought to do. I knew what he was thinking, and I started thinking the same. I worked out how much we'd each get if we divided the Cross three ways, and though I've never pinched anything else in my life, I couldn't have said no to Brindle if I'd known I was due for a spell of prison the next day for agreeing.'

It was easy to visualize the scene. A fortune, and one small, negative act of dishonesty, and it was theirs.

'We all stared at the diamonds in Brindle's hand. Blair's brother said we daren't keep anything because Blair would give us away when he recovered consciousness. Brindle kept on stroking the diamonds and said we didn't have to worry. The police didn't know Blair had stolen the Cross—it wasn't until he'd been inside for some time that the word got around to them, and although they afterwards tried to pin it on him, they never got anywhere—and since the owner had been very badly injured there was a hell of a serious charge waiting; at that time it looked as though it could easily become murder. When Blair discovered he'd lost the Cross he'd have to remain quiet because if he talked he'd be laying himself open for ten times as much trouble as he was already in.'

'Trust the lawyer to work that one out.'

Johnson nodded. 'He was as quick as a flash, had thought it all out before us two had got over the shock of looking at a fortune. Then Brindle said the one word, "Well?" I stared at the brother, he stared at me, and there wasn't any doubt. Brindle slipped the Cross into his pocket, told me to report that Blair had been taken ill. Then he left.'

'Was your story accepted without question?'

'A doctor was called for, and by the time he got there, Blair was regaining consciousness. He heard me tell the doctor how he'd come over dizzy, fallen sideways, and smacked his chin on the cell wall. Blair looked at me when I'd finished saying my piece.'

'That probably wasn't very comforting?'

'He knew what had happened even before he reached up to his neck to check whether the Cross was still there or not. When he found nothing, he kept quiet.'

'I take it he had something to say after the doctor had gone?'

'He asked me where the Cross was. I told him I didn't know what he was talking about. He just looked at me and said I must be tired of life. Made me feel as though someone were walking up and down my backbone.'

'The feeling wasn't unpleasant enough to make you give back the Cross?'

'I couldn't have returned it if it had been the devil calling for it. When a poor man sees money like I'd just seen, nothing else matters.'

Johnson looked at the whisky bottle, then at his empty glass, made up his mind, and poured out a second drink for himself. This he finished before he continued speaking. 'I left Blair. He was called into Court later that day and was sent off for trial at the Assizes. Like Brindle had said, there was never a word from him about the Milton Cross.'

'When did you make the distribution of the diamonds?'

'I met Brindle that night, and Blair's brother, Dukes. Brindle and I wanted to split up the Cross then and there. Dukes asked us what we knew about getting rid of stolen jewels and when we said it wasn't anything, he wanted to take the Cross, sell it, and give us the money later. We weren't having any of that and said so. Neither of us trusted him. He claimed we'd probably blow the whole thing sky high by being caught, but it didn't make no difference. We broke up the Cross and divided it.'

'Not exactly, I take it.'

Johnson became angry. 'There were thirteen stones and Brindle was suggesting the largest one in the centre could be counted as being worth three of the smaller ones, when Dukes pulled a gun and told us he was taking his share of the smaller stones and also the big one, because it was his brother who'd done all the work and the rewards ought to stay in the family. There weren't nothing we could do about it.'

'A double-cross played on top of a double-cross! Dukes knew you'd keep quiet about his "theft" because you daren't do otherwise; besides, you'd still got four of the smaller diamonds each.'

'We'd trusted him, and look what we got for it.' Johnson spoke heatedly, and it was clear the memory still rankled.

Blackshirt smiled grimly. When thieves fell out, the resulting happenings were inclined to be tortuous. 'Was that how things ended up?' he asked.

'It was. Never saw Dukes again, and Brindle only waited around long enough to tell me what would happen when Blair came out of prison. I told him I didn't need no warning about that.'

'What precautions against being found by Blair did you take?'

'Quit my job in the police, disappeared without telling anyone where I was going and bought this place.'

'Why didn't you change your name?'

'Blair wasn't due out for a long time and I reckoned I'd move again and might get a new name then.'

'His death saved you a lot of trouble.'

'It must have done for all of us.'

And that, thought the cracksman, was as pleasant an epitaph as the dead man was ever likely to get. He returned to the subject. 'Who's after the Cross now?'

'You.'

'I didn't do the killings.'

'That's what—— Don't know nothing.' Johnson had been about to make a tactless remark.

'Have you thought that whoever it is, sooner or later he'll be after you?'

He shrugged his shoulders. 'Won't be able to find me.'

'I managed,' remarked Blackshirt drily.

It was strange Johnson had not before realized that fact, and the meaning of it in relation to the murders of the Judge and Brindle. His face became drained of colour. 'You only managed through what the police knew.'

'What I did, another can.'

'There aren't two Blackshirts.'

'At the moment that's precisely what there are,' replied the cracksman, treating the statement literally, and ignoring the compliment.

Johnson had the kind of mind which, if it could seize on an answer that brought comfort, did so, and refused to countenance the possibility that there might be other answers less cheering. 'He won't find me,' he stated definitely.

'I hope not.'

Johnson poured himself out a third whisky. When he had filled his glass there was little liquid left in the bottle. 'There's nothing more I can tell you.'

'Don't overlook the most important fact of all.'

'What's that?'

'What happened to the four diamonds you had.'

Johnson lifted the glass to his lips, drank so quickly some of the liquid trickled down the right-hand side of his mouth to his chin, from where it dripped to the sheet. 'I sold them—where the hell d'you think I got all the money from? My aunt?' The alcohol had quite suddenly taken effect, making him confident, loud, slightly belligerent.

'Sold them to whom?'

'You've had your value for money.'

Blackshirt leaned forward. 'I haven't heard enough, as yet, Johnson, to stop me planting a few strange plants about this house.'

Johnson swore, finished the drink, lit a cigarette. He tried to summon up the courage to resist his inquisitor, but the whisky failed him. 'Bloke called Amos—he went through the local court once on a charge of receiving. We all knew he was as guilty as hell, but couldn't pin it on him, so he got away. I remembered where he lived in London, went and saw him. He gave me a fair price for the diamonds, all things considered.'

Blackshirt stood up. 'I can't think of anything more to ask you, but if ever I do I'll drop in and have another word with you.'

'Why don't you drop dead?' replied Johnson—to himself.

*

Blackshirt made his way out of the house.

Some of the picture was how clear. The murderer, in following up the trail of the diamonds, had overtaken Brindle and so claimed four of them. The murderer had also previously mistakenly believed the Judge to have been involved, hence the reason the Judge had been tortured—in an effort to make him disclose something he had no means of knowing—and then killed.

He stood outside the house and thought about his future steps, and knew that at last he had a tangible lead to follow. So cheered was he by the knowledge, he remembered that it was just possible the two men were still guarding the alarm, not to try and trap Blackshirt who obviously would not return, but to see if Johnson had any intention of breaking out.

He moved forward. As he neared where the two constables had been before, he came to a halt, listened. He heard the faint rustle of clothing brushing against clothing, then the sudden sound as someone blew heavily through his nose to clear it.

He approached the unfortunate men.

Chapter Nine

OTTO SPEYER coughed harshly, gasped for breath, lit a cigarette and inhaled, which immediately made him cough the more.

'You ought to give it up,' observed Blackshirt.

'As I've said many times, give up all that one should, and there is nothing pleasant left in life.' Having made which pronouncement, Speyer coughed for at least a minute and the tears ran down his cheeks. He crossed the room, poured himself out a drink which he swallowed as quickly as though it were medicine. 'I'm getting on in years,' he said mournfully. 'One of these days I shall retire and buy myself a place in the country where I can while away my remaining years in peace.'

Blackshirt laughed immoderately.

'What's so amusing?'

'Your sad choice of words, Otto, not to mention the thought of you beneath the cherry-blossom, dangling a shy young grandchild on each chubby knee.'

'I see nothing funny in such picture,' snapped Speyer angrily.

'My apologies.'

'Do you think me incapable of sitting beneath cherry-blossom?'

Blackshirt decided it was time to try to be diplomatic. 'What about all your business?'

'Yes,' admitted the other after a long pause, in rather a wistful voice, 'I should hate to leave it.'

'Not even at a time when it's not doing so well?'

'It's doing very well,' snapped Otto, before he realized that he had said completely the wrong thing, since the cracksman might think higher prices could well be paid for the jewellery he brought to the fence. 'For a small business that has to struggle all the time to keep its head above water,' he added hastily, to try and cover his mistake.

Blackshirt might not have heard him. 'Funny you missed some of the biggest stuff that's been shifted for a long time. Not been feeling up to the mark, Otto?'

'What are you talking about?'

'Not like you to miss the big tricks.'

Speyer showed signs of the angry impatience within him. 'What have I missed? Who's tried to cheat me?' His definition of "cheating" was rather enlarged from ordinary standards, since it included anyone in London—and sometimes beyond—who tried to sell stolen jewellery above a certain value to anyone but himself.

'Someone else offering bigger prices? Money transcends loyalties these days.'

'Where, who, what? . . . Blackshirt, tell me. Has someone bought the Bathurst pearl, or is it the Welsh ruby?'

'The Milton Cross, Otto.'

The fence was expecting anything but that answer, and it was some time before he regained sufficient composure to ask the question that was foremost in his mind. 'Has it gone elsewhere?'

'Part of it has, for a certainty.'

Speyer's rather chubby fingers slowly began to work. The deliberation of his action made it an ominous one. 'How great a part?'

'Four of the thirteen diamonds.'

'Only four?'

'That's the number I know have passed through other hands.'

'Where are the rest?'

'I can't pin-point them for sure, but I'm working on the belief that Blair's brother has five, the murderer the remaining four.'

'Who handled the four you first mentioned?'

'Does the name of Amos ring a bell?'

'Amos,' repeated Speyer slowly. The fingers of his two hands joined together and suddenly strained against each other. 'How do you know?'

'Straight from the man who sold the diamonds to him.'

'Why are you telling me?'

'I want to know what Amos did with them.'

'He has been a very stupid man.'

'There's another thing you can find out—what happened to Blair's brother, Dukes?'

'That's a sticky assignment, Blackshirt.'

'Good one to carry out successfully.'

'It'll take time—if it can be done at all.'

'You can offer a large sum to help people's tongues clack.'

'When will you bring me the money?'

Blackshirt laughed. 'You can provide it, Otto, as a special favour.'

'Favour for what?' grumbled the other. When forced to spend money, sentiment, to him, became an unknown word.

*

Amos listened to the message that had come to him by ways more devious than the post but much quicker. He licked his lips. 'What the hell does he want?' he demanded.

'Don't know,' answered the bringer of glad tidings.

'He can whistle if he thinks I'm going to come running the second he calls.'

'He don't like to be kept waiting.'

'I'll suit myself when and if I turn up.'

'Tired of life?'

Amos was not tired of life, and having shown a modicum of defiance, he hastily started on his way to see Speyer. As he made his way through the dingy streets he wondered what the call presaged, became more and more nervous.

Amos climbed the steep stairs, knocked at the door, entered the room. The lighting was dim, but not so dim that he could not observe the expression on Speyer's face. He felt more nervous.

'Sit down,' said Speyer.

Amos did so. Seeking to ease the all-but-overwhelming feeling of apprehension, he searched in his coat pocket for a packet of cigarettes. Speyer forestalled him, pushed across a box made of carved ivory.

'Been busy?' asked Speyer, a little later.

'Not very,' replied Amos tactfully.

'Nothing very big around these days, is there?'

'Not since you took over,' was the unusually spirited reply.

Speyer accepted the words as a compliment and smiled. People said he had a brutal nature. That was not true. He was a business man to whom the usual standards of business efficiency applied, and by this token it was his duty to remove any competitor who came into direct competition with him; the fact that such removal was liable to be more permanent than in most cases was just one of the little distinguishing differences about his particular business. 'No sign of the Bathurst pearl?' he asked.

Amos relaxed. It seemed that his earlier reading of the expression on Speyer's face was grossly at fault. Speyer wanted help and had rightly decided to approach Amos for it. 'Haven't heard anything. Like me to put my ear to the ground?'

Speyer seemed about to answer at some length, but he checked himself and finally said only, 'Don't bother.'

'No bother at all. . . . I'll tell you straight, I've always thought you and me could work together just fine.'

'Could we?'

'That's a hundred and ten per cent right.'

'Maybe you think we ought to try a partnership?'

'I most certainly do,' replied an enthusiastic Amos. 'Man, in a couple of years we'll be sitting in the luxury flat in Easy Street.'

'You would suggest a full co-operation between us?'

'Complete right up to the hilt.'

'Good,' said Otto, in a smooth voice. 'Then to cement this newly formed business association, perhaps you'll tell me to whom you sold the Milton Cross diamonds.'

Amos underwent a certain obvious change. His smile, noticeable for the resplendent array of gold-filled teeth, lost much of its freshness, finally wilted. His mouth became dry. 'The Milton Cross diamonds,' he whispered.

'That's right.'

'Don't know nothing about them.'

'I distinctly remember,' said Speyer in a quiet, friendly voice, 'sending out word that they were to come to me.'

'I don't know nothing about them.'

'You bought four.'

'I've never seen the colour of them. Who's the ruddy liar who says I have?'

'I am,' said a new voice.

Amos turned round. A shadow moved forward, gathered substance and outline. There could be no mistaking the black shirt and hood. 'Blackshirt!'

'Good evening.'

'What are you doing here? What do you both want?' His voice became shrill as a feeling of panic flooded through him.

'The diamonds.'

He made as though to get up, realized there could be no thought of escape, sank back into the chair. He stared at the black figure. 'I didn't know you was interested or I wouldn't have touched them, not if a host of angels had asked me on bended knees.'

Blackshirt said nothing.

'This bloke offered them to me. I bought them. It's as simple as that.'

'Had you forgotten what I'd said?' snapped Otto.

Amos discovered there was room in his mind for only one great fear at a time. He ignored Speyer. 'I gave him a fair price, then sold them for a small profit.'

'Which was how long after you'd bought them?'

'A couple of months. A chap on the Continent paid good money for good stuff.'

'The name?'

Amos hesitated, but a further glance at the black figure which stood silently before him decided him. He gave the name of the man to whom he had sold the diamonds.

*

As Roberts packed the suitcase, Verrell paced the room. He picked up the cup of coffee from the small table, drank the contents. The liquid had been too hot, and the burning feeling hurried down his throat.

How much time had he? It was impossible to estimate beyond the certainty that it was very little. The killer had the diamonds of Brindle. He might, or might not, have Dukes'. Taking a gloomy view of things, that left only Johnson's diamonds to be gained before the killer completed his task. And taking an even gloomier view, might he not already have those of Johnson? If that was so, then . . . There was no point in being that pessimistic. If one was, then one must recognize that Blackshirt was forever to be classified as a murderer, since the day that the killer no longer pursued the jewels was the day he could no longer be traced.

Verrell stopped pacing the room. 'What's the time?'

'Ten minutes before we need leave, sir,' answered Roberts.

He noted the disapproval in the other's voice. Roberts thought he had become too impatient and would fatally endanger himself because of that impatience.

He lit a cigarette. What were his chances? That was anybody's guess. If he could secure but one of the diamonds, the battle would be waged on more level terms, because the killer would be forced to venture into Blackshirt's territory to try to gain that one.

But right then it seemed unlikely that he, Blackshirt, could succeed even to that extent.

What success would Otto have in tracing Dukes Blair? Were the police still firmly convinced that it was the cracksman who was the murderer? If he failed to secure any of the diamonds, was there really nothing he could do?

'I think you have everything, sir.'

'Right you are.'

'Shall I take the case down?'

'Yes, please.'

Roberts would accompany him to the airport to bring the car back. In a handful of hours he would be in Copenhagen, searching for the man to whom Amos had sold the diamonds. For once the thought of travelling abroad did not fill his mind with pleasurable anticipation. This journey was too much in the nature of a business one; too much depended on its successful outcome.

He left the room, walked down the corridor, then descended the short flight of stairs that led down to the open front-door. He crossed the pavement, sat down behind the steering wheel of his Austin-Healey, started the engine and listened with approval to the harsh crackle of the exhaust note. There was little that was standard about this car—including the driver, was the comment added by one nervous passenger shortly after having been driven by him.

He let out the clutch and they began to move away from the pavement. Roberts eased himself into a more secure position in the passenger's seat. It was not that he had any fears—those had been blown from him many years ago—it was merely a prudent move to be within easy reach of the grab-rail.

*

Verrell stood in the square and stared about him. He liked, and disliked, Copenhagen. Unfortunately, it was always so flattered in posters and travel books it never quite came up to expectations which immediately engendered a certain amount of annoyance.

He entered a café and ordered coffee, regretted the fact that it was not the general custom to sit out on the pavement as it was in other parts of the Continent. No doubt such action annoyed the logical and tidy mind of the Danish people. The pavement was for walking on.

He thought about the man he had telephoned. He had mentioned Speyer, and that had been some form of an introduction, but not a sufficient one. The man had insisted that he must meet and see Verrell, learn at first-hand precisely what it was the other wanted, and since he was not free until that evening, that was the earliest time at which the meeting could take place. Verrell had protested, but it had been useless, and at last he had had to agree. The man had been in no way astonished. It had been logical to agree.

The coffee arrived at his table, but its smell was more attractive than its taste. He sighed. Half the fun of going abroad was in the eating and the drinking.

He spent the day as a good tourist should, visiting the museums if they were open, which all too frequently they were not, the shopping area, a brewery, and seeing the famous mermaid, a pathetic figure, lost amidst her surroundings.

He ate dinner in one of the more luxurious restaurants, enjoyed the cooking because it was more cosmopolitan than regional. Later he made his way to the club at which the meeting was to take place.

The main room, with sunken dance floor in the centre, was empty of anyone but several bored waiters. Verrell checked with his watch to make certain that by some peculiar mistake he had not arrived two hours earlier than the suggested time, found, as he had thought, it was nearly midnight. He stood where he was, and since he could not be ignored for ever, eventually was shown to a table. The wine bill was brought. Beer was cheap; anything else was not. He chose beer and the waiter was plainly disgusted that a foreigner should have learned the customs so quickly.

Verrell leaned back and looked about him. He was still the only person present, and, had he been told he had entered the inner sanctum of an undertakers' convention, would have accepted the information and believed it.

A man and a woman entered, sat down at the nearest table to the door, ordered beer. The band, until then either tuning their instruments or sleeping, realized custom had arrived and livened up. A man announced the first half of the cabaret.

The cabaret lasted twelve and a half minutes, and at the end of that time it was difficult to say who was the more dispirited—the three members of the public, or the troupe of dancing girls, all of whom were unluckily aware of the limits of their capabilities. They bowed at the completion of the act, left. The band resumed its former occupations, the dance floor remained empty.

Verrell felt it was time someone introduced a little feverish gaiety and ordered another beer, lit another cigarette. He hoped his actions would not attract the attentions of any Watch Committee.

A man, so enormously fat he sent before him an immediate mental picture of the floor giving way, entered, looked round. The head waiter awoke and leapt into action, spoke to the newcomer, ceremoniously ushered him across to Verrell's table.

'Good evening,' said the man, in near-perfect English.

Verrell stood up, shook hands, and was amazed to note how completely his own hand became lost in that of the other.

The newcomer sat down slowly. The chair beneath him creaked twice, but as he finally rested the whole of his weight on it, it remained intact. He overflowed the seat of the chair to such an extent it was as though he had to balance himself on it.

'Beer,' ordered the man. The waiter nodded, left.

The huge head turned and the eyes studied Verrell. They were lifeless, as though they belonged to a dead man. 'How are you enjoying our wonderful city?'

'Very much.'

'Of course, you have not come at the right time. You should be here during the height of the season—then, all is gaiety.'

'I'm sure it must be.'

The beer arrived. The huge man's likes were evidently well known, for he was presented with a tankard that must have contained a quart of beer. He lifted this to his lips, began to swallow. Fascinated, Verrell watched the smooth action that resulted in at least half the beer vanishing in a handful of seconds.

'I believe we have business to discuss?' Those eyes stared across the rim of the tankard.

Verrell stubbed out his cigarette. 'Maybe.'

'Why maybe?'

'We may not like each other's terms.' He spoke crisply.

The other nodded. 'That is true.' His expression became careful.

'I want information.'

'I want money. Depending on the importance of the information you seek, so my price will rise.'

'What did you do with the four diamonds from the Milton Cross?'

The man shifted the tankard back to his lips, resumed drinking. Very soon he put the empty vessel down on the table. He looked round for the waiter, signalled. The latter came to the table, took the tankard, left. 'That is not the kind of information I sell,' he said finally. 'Someone should have told you and thus saved you the trouble of coming all this way only to meet a refusal.'

'I was told that a good price secured anything.'

'My clients must be able to trust me. If they know I remain silent, they can do just that.'

Verrell leaned forward. 'I shall gain the information I require,' he said quietly. 'Whether I buy it amicably, or gain it forcibly, I leave to you.'

The waiter returned with the tankard. The huge man lifted it to his mouth and drank, as though taking part in a ritual. He was greatly angered, for it was a long time since any man had spoken to him as this Englishman had done. 'You are either very brave or very foolish to speak to me like that.'

'I intend to know what you did with the diamonds.'

Seated opposite the other, Verrell was dwarfed and all but reduced to doll-like proportions. Yet when he spoke in his quiet voice he seemed to match the other, size for size.

'Sold them,' said the fat man.

'To whom?'

The tankard was raised up and the last drop was drained from it. Then it was replaced on the table. 'Perhaps I do something very strange and unusual and sell this information—it will be expensive.'

'But not exorbitant.' Verrell spoke mockingly. The silent battle of wills had been won by him, and he did not intend that that fact should be forgotten.

'What kind of money?'

'Are there many kinds?'

'You must know the meaning of my words.'

'What kind are you usually paid in when you act the part of a stool-pigeon?'

The deliberate insult fanned the anger of the fat man to choking bitterness. He wore a gun in a shoulder holster and for several seconds wildly wondered if he dare use it. Reason returned to his mind, and so did the riling knowledge that no matter what the circumstances, he would never dare draw on this Englishman, because he was afraid. He took a handkerchief from his pocket, wiped his forehead and then the back of his neck. 'One thousand dollars, paid in dollars.'

Verrell laughed.

'Very well, then; the equivalent in pounds sterling.'

Verrell picked up the wine list to check if there were any drink he might order which was more attractive than the beer, and which did not cost a fortune.

'Nine hundred—take it or leave it.'

Verrell dropped the wine list. 'One hundred pounds.'

The fat man sneered. 'Chicken feed.'

'Better that than nothing but trouble. . . . To whom did you sell the jewels?'

The fat man hesitated, and because he did so, knew that he had agreed to the terms.

Verrell took the money from his pocket, handed it to the other. He listened carefully to what was said, then prepared to leave. A waiter rushed up and expressed astonishment that the Englishman should be leaving so early, more especially since the second half of the cabaret was about to begin. Verrell increased his speed of departure.

*

While most of the city retired to bed at an early hour, no doubt worn out by the many and varied amusements, the taxis were always on duty, and although it might take a certain amount of effort to awaken the driver, perseverance usually had its reward and a grunt would indicate that the passenger had been accepted.

Verrell was driven out to one of the more pleasant suburbs along a broad road flanked with shops, which finally came to a T junction. The taxi turned left, continued for two hundred yards, made a U turn, drew up against the pavement. Verrell checked on the amount the meter showed, added a reasonable tip, paid the money. The driver seemed disgusted that his tip was only fifty per cent more than a native of the city would have given him, but after a quick look at his fare's determined features, refrained from saying what had been in his mind.

The taxi left. Verrell crossed the pavement until against the wooden fence of the house, took the case from his pocket, lit a cigarette.

He studied the road. No car was parked within sight, no uniform was in evidence—he found it difficult to distinguish the policeman from the candlestick maker—nor were any other pedestrians about. He began to walk back toward the T junction.

A car came round the corner, rattling as the wheels momentarily caught in the tram-lines. Two men walked out of the grounds of what was some form of club and sang and swayed their way past him.

The house was on its own, having on one side a church, on the other a ten-foot-tall wooden fence. He paused, ostensibly to stamp out his cigarette, and made a last check. All was quiet. Satisfied, he continued to walk along the pavement until level with the end of the small garden-space where he came within the deep shadow of a large tree growing in the church grounds, but whose branches spread wide and far.

He crossed the shallow wall with one swift movement that was soundless. An observer would, had he been watching, have been uncertain whether he had seen anything or not, and when there was no further movement would have assumed the latter assumption to be the correct one.

The windows facing Blackshirt were large, being both tall and wide, with the two sides meeting at the top in a graceful arch. They opened down the centre, and he wondered what kind of lock secured them. He noted that this side of the house was in deep shadow, while the other must be almost directly within the radius of a street-light.

He checked that hood and gloves were secure, crossed to the wall of the house, chose the nearest window. He took a very thin strip of pliable metal from his belt of tools, inserted one end of this between the two halves of the window, drew the metal upwards and felt it strike the catch. He increased the pressure, but failed to force the window, and after one more attempt decided it would be necessary to cut away sufficient of the glass to enable him to reach inside and manually release the catch.

He took his glass-cutter and began to work on the window. For once he did not move in complete silence, and at one point he half-tripped and struck the window-frame with his fist—there was a dull thud, which, in the quiet of the night, contained the force of a miniature explosion. He stopped work and listened, but all was quiet.

*

Jorgens waited. He sat by the light which had been tilted so that it would shine directly on the window the moment it was switched on. In his right hand he held an automatic pistol.

Although he would have jeered at anyone who told him he was excited, such was the case. His grip about the pistol was tight, and his finger pressed on the trigger—he had but to flick over the safety catch with his thumb, and once again he would hear the harsh crackle as it fired, would smell the acrid fumes.

He laughed silently to himself. He had been warned and had thereupon used his head. He had judged the visit would be unannounced and that the intruder would break in wherever was the weakest part of the house. Jorgens knew that the long windows in the shadow of the tree were a "natural."

He had denied himself the luxury of a cigarette, although the urge to smoke had become greater and greater. The scent of the smoke, long after the household had gone to sleep, would alert the intruder. That such precaution was not to be wasted became clear when from the sounds beyond he knew someone was trying to force an entry by way of the second window.

He had worked out precisely what would happen. It was strange how circumscribed were the minds of criminals. Given a certain set of circumstances, each and every one of them reacted in the same predictable way.

The man would break into the room in which Jorgens sat, because that was obviously the way to enter. Jorgens was not yet certain whether he would kill; was the pleasure worth the risk that the shot, or shots, would attract attention?

He had heard nothing for some while now. Evidently the man outside was waiting to make certain that all the noise he had so far caused had raised no one. That suited Jorgens. He was a man who received little joy from life, but to have the choice to kill was a great pleasure. The longer that pleasure was deferred, the more he could savour it.

He sat, gun in hand, feeling the hard knot of excitement deep within him. He had finally decided to kill. The man deserved to die because of his lack of imagination.

'Waiting for someone?' asked Blackshirt quietly.

Jorgens felt the shock of surprise flood through him. His mind seemed to be cut off from the world, suspended in time, timeless.

Light from a torch covered and outlined him, and he thought of it as the force of death.

How did the mocking voice come to be behind him? The intruder was still outside, trying to break in through the window that every criminal would choose; he, Jorgens, had heard the sounds of the attempted entry. How, then, came the man to be in the house?

'I made a noise to attract and hold your attention,' said Blackshirt, as though he had heard the questions in the other man's mind, 'then went round to the far side of the house and broke in.'

So simple! Jorgens felt contemptuous fury for his own stupidity. It was he who had acted in circumscribed manner, because he had relied on the intruder conforming to pattern. Imagining himself the stalker had resulted in his being the stalked.

'Drop the gun.'

Dare he turn? Shoot to silence the man who had proved him, Jorgens, to be a fool? He dropped the gun to the floor. He dare not.

His hands were seized and tied behind the chair. He tried to damp down fear, but could not. There was little light, and each shadow had grown its own threat, all the more potent because he had not yet seen the man behind him. Death had been summoned to the room, and . . .

'Where are the diamonds?'

'What diamonds?' he answered, in a voice that dipped as he swallowed hastily.

'The ones I have come here to recover.'

'I . . . I haven't got them any longer.'

'That's rather unfortunate.'

He answered in Danish, realized he would not be understood, reverted to English which he spoke fluently. 'It's the truth.'

'Why were you sitting here with a gun? Guarding nothing?'

'I thought you might be along, and . . .'

'You were warned—by telephone?'

Jorgens licked his lips. 'Yes. . . . I haven't got the diamonds,' he said suddenly.

'Your denial is becoming monotonous.'

'I had them. I bought them a few years ago. Recently, I had great need of money and was forced to sell them.'

'To whom?'

'I tried to sell in this country, but no one would offer me the price. Then a contact told me a man in England wanted to buy them and was prepared to pay a fair price.'

'Who was it?'

'I don't know.'

'Who was he?'

'For God's sake, I'm telling the truth—you don't ask for passports in this kind of business.'

'What did he look like?'

Jorgens tried to remember, but his memory was distorted and his words described nobody.

'Through whom did you make the contact?' demanded Blackshirt.

'A man I knew.'

'Knew?'

'He was killed in a car accident.'

'Convenient!'

'It's the truth. It's the truth.'

Blackshirt wondered if the fat man had known that Jorgens did not have the diamonds. The question was not one that concerned him for long, since the point was immaterial. What mattered was to try to check the rest of what had been said. The story had been too vague, too unfinished. . . . But was not that the way of life?

Two and a half hours later Blackshirt was as certain as he could be that he had heard the truth. A lengthy interrogation had taught him nothing more, and a search of the house had been equally negative.

As he stared at the bound figure immediately before he left the house, he suddenly felt very tired and dispirited.

Chapter Ten

'WHAT happened, Blackshirt?' asked Speyer eagerly and expectantly. The fence had a love of beautiful jewels that could be a source of much distress to him when it came to the time to sell them. His only consolation at such moments was the money he received in exchange.

Blackshirt sat down on the edge of the table after he had moved to one side the small wood carving of Indian origin. 'I'll give you one guess.'

'Then you have them! Let me see them—I have heard it said they are the finest diamonds of their size in the world.'

'Wrong.'

'You haven't returned without them?' Speyer's astonishment was comical. Although he tried to conceal the fact, he had always regarded the cracksman as infallible, and it came as a shock to discover that this was not so.

'I had a pleasant journey, admired the country, enjoyed myself—but that was all.' He spoke ironically, and his hearer was left uncertain as to whether he had enjoyed any part of his trip.

'The man I told you to contact, did he not assist?'

'He did all that was asked of him—and more—after a certain amount of persuasion. He gave me the name of the one who had bought the jewels. I saw this latter man, but he had had itchy fingers and sold them again.'

'Where?'

'England.'

Speyer's thick features gathered into an ugly expression. 'Impossible! Maybe once the diamonds are dealt with and I am not consulted; that couldn't happen twice.'

'It did.'

'Who?

'Jorgens couldn't say. To complicate matters, the in-between man is dead.'

Speyer relaxed slightly. The right ending to the story had been reached. 'That's good,' he said unthinkingly.

'Like hell it is! Where do we start looking for the diamonds?'

'As you say, where?' He shrugged his shoulders with an angry gesture, lit a cigarette.

'I don't know the answer, Otto.'

'Does it matter that much? It would be nice to gain all of the diamonds, but if you can't, half of them will not make too bad a present.'

'Otto, if I don't get to them first, I remain a murderer in the eyes of the police and public.'

Speyer flicked his cigarette, although no ash had formed. 'To be so sensitive creates a great number of difficulties.'

Blackshirt's voice became harsh. 'That's my affair.'

'Of course, of course.' He hesitated, then continued speaking. 'I was trying to point out something that has been troubling me for a long while. I know, Blackshirt, how much it angers you to be called a murderer. Naturally, you all but break your neck in the effort to destroy such appellation, but, as you've already found out, since you must of necessity be one jump behind the murderer, you're battling under near-impossible difficulties. He moves first, and knows you must follow.' Speyer, seeing Blackshirt was about to speak, held up his hand. 'I know that so far you've fought your way clear. But luck is always eager to run in an opposite direction, Blackshirt, and then you are either exposed or dead. . . . I'm saying this because I don't want that to be the ending. Rest content that presumably the murderer doesn't know your real identity, and therefore if you stay out of this from now on he can bring no harm to you.'

'I wish I could, Otto.'

'What stops you?'

'You know as well as I do.'

'A name is not worth a life.'

'I think it is.'

Speyer stubbed out his cigarette, stood up, crossed to the far wall where was the cocktail cabinet. He opened it, poured out for himself a large glassful of whisky. He added a suspicion of soda, but no more. 'If you were killed I should feel as though I had lost a friend,' he said quietly.

'Despite the past?'

'Perhaps you have come here and demanded four times as much money for jewellery as anyone else would dare, and perhaps sometimes I've been stupid enough to pay it. That is business. I was referring to friendship which lives outside business.'

Blackshirt stared at Speyer and knew the fence was stating the truth. It was a strange thought that he was capable of any such feeling—most of those who knew him would have sworn the Sphinx had more red blood in it than did he. 'I'd also be very sorry to lose the connection,' said Blackshirt.

Speyer lit another cigarette. 'Then perhaps you will break off this engagement with the murderer, who must eventually win.'

'No.'

He sighed. 'You are obstinate to the point of stupidity.'

'I'm sorry you don't rate my capabilities more highly.'

'I rate no man's higher.'

'Shall I see you at my funeral?'

Speyer swore. 'Why will you not take my advice seriously?'

Blackshirt's voice hardened. 'I know how the cards are dealt, and having been on the receiving end of things, I know what stakes the loser will have to pay. But acknowledgement doesn't mean I wear black before I have to.'

The fence finished what was in the glass, poured himself out another drink. 'Damned if I can see the logic in that,' he muttered, uncertain whether there were meant to be any anyway.

They were silent until Blackshirt asked, 'Have you located Dukes Blair?'

Speyer returned to the chair behind the desk, sat down. 'I have not. Despite everything I have done, and that is all that can be, I have learned nothing. Money has proved to be as useless as threats. I have followed up any trail that had so much as a dusty beginning, but it has been useless.'

'No hints?'

'None.'

'Helpful!'

'What will you do now?'

'Try, and keep on trying, to trace him.'

Speyer shook his head slowly. 'I hope you never find him,' he said finally.

*

Superintendent Ashley stared at the ash-tray. It was a large one, but was filled by cigarette stubs. They represented what he had smoked in the past twenty-four hours. He knew the habit was harmful to him, and quite frequently he gave it up. Usually it was his wife's complaints which drove him back to the vice. She claimed he was unbelievably unbearable at such moments.

He jerked his mind away from that problem and transferred it to another. The murders of Parlant and Brindle were still unsolved, or rather, the murderer had not been caught, which in this particular instance was a means of saying the same thing in a different way. He leaned back in his chair. Although there was still room for doubt in his mind if he allowed it to form, he was near enough certain that Blackshirt was the murderer. Why a man who had for so long eschewed violence should suddenly take to it in its most savage form was a question some of the psycho-gentlemen might like to answer. But Blackshirt had taken to murder and that was that, and he, Ashley, was supposed to capture him. The kind of task that spelled out premature grey hairs and unclaimed pension.

He was surprised to find that a cigarette was fastened to his upper lip. He had no memory of taking it from a packet, or of lighting it. He moved it from his lip so that he could inhale, used his tongue to return it to his lip.

Detective-Sergeant Hooper came into the room, sat down, groaned. 'Me dogs are killing me.'

'For heaven's sake, what the devil are you talking about?'

'I'm crippled.'

'Leave the medical report for some other time. Have you learned anything?'

Hooper sighed. 'From Johnson, nothing. He's scared, but not quite scared enough.'

'You ought to have got it out of him long before now.'

'How? I can't threaten him with anything, and on my salary I couldn't bribe a pauper.'

Ashley smacked right fist into the palm of left hand. 'Blackshirt found out something, he must have done, which means there's something to learn and Johnson was mixed up in the Cross affair. How, why, what? We've got to find the answers.'

'How?'

'Sometimes, Bill, I get an overwhelming desire to take you by the scruff of your neck and . . . If I knew how, we'd have done so a long while before now.'

'Every time Johnson sees me he just laughs in my face.'

'I'd make him laugh some if he were still in the force.'

'Can't we pin anything on him?'

'We've sniffed round that money he inherited until we've all got sore noses, and what good's it done? Everything's so legal it stinks!'

'I wonder just how much he knows.'

'Enough to land him in for a good stretch, I'll bet a packet.'

'Grim to see just how much better dishonesty pays than honesty.'

'If it's taken you all these years to discover that, you're an even worse policeman than I thought,' snapped Ashley. He felt a burning sensation in his lip, removed the cigarette stub, dropped it into the ash-tray.

'Where do we go from here?' asked Hooper, a little later.

'Home.'

Hooper looked up at the clock. 'Didn't realize it was that late.'

'I did. Had to 'phone the wife and say I'd be late for the meal—that's the sixth time in ten days.'

Hooper stood up, paced the floor-space between the two desks. 'What's really driving me round the bend is the fact that for once we know who, and why; yet we can't do anything about it.'

'It's annoying the A.C. too.'

'Again?'

The Superintendent wearily nodded his head. 'Claims the lot of us would make excellent filing clerks.'

'I'd like to see what he could——' Hooper's words were interrupted by the telephone. He lifted the receiver, listened to what was said, replied only twice and then in monosyllables. Finally he replaced the receiver.

'Well?' asked Ashley.

'Another knife murder.'

The Superintendent was instantly alert and had lost the lethargic air that he assumed when deep in thought, an attitude that was inclined to make people who did not know him misjudge him as a not very astute man. 'Let's have the details.'

'Only the initial report has come in so far. Traynor's on the job and thought it was just possible this was connected with our two cases.'

'Because a knife was used?'

Hooper shook his head. 'The man was beaten up, then tortured, before he was killed.'

Ashley stood up. 'Give my wife a tinkle and tell her I won't be back at all, will you?' He left the room.

Hooper stared at the door through which the other had gone. He supposed he would have to deliver the same message to his own home. He felt sad. Wives never seemed to understand there was such a thing as legitimate business carried on in the evenings.

*

The neighbourhood was colourless. It was neither rich nor poor, artistic nor downright ugly. Some of the houses were clean, some were not. Some of the gardens were well kept, some were filled with weeds.

A policeman guarded a door in one of the streets and the many people who had gathered expectantly watched the constable. Their interest increased when a police car drew up and two men climbed out and entered the house. The watchers gazed after the car as it drove slowly away. Nothing was too insignificant.

Ashley met Traynor in the room to the right of the front door. 'Thanks for giving me the wink, Ted.'

Superintendent Traynor looked up. 'May be a wild goose chase for you, but I thought it was worth the effort.'

'Right now, I'd chase moonbeams if I could find any.'

'Don't envy you your job.'

'No one does.' Ashley took a cigarette case from his pocket, offered it around. 'What's the set-up here?'

Traynor waited to reply until he was certain that the tip of the cigarette was well alight. 'I don't think there's much more to it than I told the sergeant over the telephone. Chap came round here to see North, knocked on the front door and received no answer. He noticed the milk hadn't been taken in, nor had the newspaper, so got in touch with the police. That soon brought me in on the scene, and when I saw the set-up I reckoned you might be interested.'

'Thanks.'

'You don't sound all that pleased.'

'I'm not.'

Traynor grinned sympathetically. 'From what I've heard, I can understand.'

Ashley hastened to return the subject to essentials. 'When was death?'

'Maybe twenty-four hours ago.'

'Where is the body?'

'Next door. We can go in as soon as the photographers have finished. Think this could be sewn up with the other murders?'

Ashley shook his head. 'Your guess is as good as mine at this stage. Hope it's no relation, then someone else beside me can worry himself stupid.'

They entered the next room four minutes later. The body was still in the chair in which it had been bound. Ashley noted the wounds, was surprised to find that even after the number of years he had been a policeman he could still be shocked. He walked round to the back of the chair. 'Same way of lashing the arms and legs,' he said. He returned to the front of the chair, stared at the face. 'Know anything about the history of the man?'

'Men are searching the place now. Chap who reported the murder said North came to the district a few years ago, never talked much but was quite well liked.'

Ashley grunted. 'Care to have the prints taken and checked with Records?'

'I was going to do that; any ideas who it is?'

He shook his head again. 'Your guess is still every bit as good as mine.' Traynor irritated him by repeatedly asking that question. He had ideas, plenty of them, and they churned about his head, but he refused to give tongue to any of them at that point.

Two hours passed, and the policemen had searched the house. The body had been removed, and for the moment all was quiet.

'Thanks again for calling me in,' said Ashley.

'I'll let you know the rest as soon as I can.'

'If you would.'

Ashley and Hooper left. On the pavements outside the house the public stood and watched. Some of them were probably the same people that had been there when the Superintendent entered. He wished he could have shown them the body of the murdered man. Then, perhaps, they would not have waited about.

*

Ashley was sleeping when the telephone by his bedside rang. He awoke and stared at the instrument with a deep dislike that came from the memory of the many times this same thing had happened. Reluctantly he pushed an arm out into the cold, lifted the receiver from its cradle. 'Yes?'

'Traynor here—hope I haven't woken you?'

He looked at his watch and noted it was not yet seven-thirty. How fatuous could a man get?

'Got some news for you.'

'Spit it out.'

'The prints of the dead man were on the files. It was Dukes Blair.'

Ashley felt as though the worst and the best had happened simultaneously. The brother of Albert Blair, the solicitor, the policeman, and the Judge. They formed a pattern, the details of which were still blurred, but the outline of which was rapidly coming into focus.

'Are you still there?' asked Traynor.

'Yes. Thanks for letting me know.'

'Help any?'

'Might do.'

'I was wondering whether the investigations into Blair's death ought to come under you?'

'Certainly not.' Ashley hurriedly said good-bye, replaced the telephone receiver. He lay back in the bed, noted with some resentment that his wife was still asleep.

Who came into the scheme, and who did not? Had the jewels all been recovered? Had Blackshirt pulled off his coup, and would he now disappear? If the jewels had been recovered, that was tantamount to saying the whole affair could be forgotten—no one would again sight the cracksman.

Ashley was a man who used his imagination, but who was not an imaginative man. Yet as he thought about Blackshirt, changed from insolent cracksman to vicious murderer, he shuddered. Who would dare prophesy where the next killing would take place?

*

By means known only to themselves the newspapers discovered the real name of the murdered man. This they printed, together with a detailed description of the wounds he had suffered.

Verrell stared at the newspaper and it made him feel that the afternoon sun was a thing of blatant ugliness, whereas before Roberts had entered the room he had been admiring it.

He wondered whether this was the moment of defeat, and, as optimistic as he usually was, could find no good reason to suppose it to be anything else. Three men had shared the diamonds. Brindle, Johnson, and Blair. The first and last named were dead, and it seemed certain the murderer had recovered the jewels; as regards Johnson, it was reasonable to suppose that the English buyer of the diamonds had been the murderer. Then the thirteen diamonds were together again and the murderer would have no further cause to appear. Blackshirt was forever to be named as the murderer.

He ate the pastry without thought and when he had swallowed the last mouthful could not have said of what type it had been—in direct contrast to normal, when he would have consciously relished it from beginning to end.

What to do? Give up, admit defeat? That was a course of conduct that was anathema to him. What was the alternative? What lead had he? What action could he take? Whatever he might do now would stand as much chance of success as a snowball salesman in hell. He welcomed odds against him; but not when they stood as they did now.

Could Otto help? There was no reason to suppose the answer to be in the affirmative. How could he pluck something from nothing any more than could Blackshirt?

Was there really nothing to do? It seemed the answer must be, nothing.

Would the police learn anything from the latest murder? It seemed doubtful. They were certain in their own minds that the cracksman was the murderer; why should they search for something to prove he were not?

Roberts entered the room. 'More coffee, sir?'

'No, thanks. . . . Read it all?'

'Yes, sir.'

'Leave you with any bright ideas?'

'None.'

'Nor me.' He stared out of the window. 'Its main effect was to make me quite certain that the battle's been lost.'

'Isn't there a chance . . .?'

'If the diamonds have been recovered by the murderer, no.'

'Have you no ideas who the murderer is?'

'Plenty, but I've been concentrating on the diamonds. Perhaps I ought to switch tracks.' There was one small tomato sandwich left on the plate, and this he ate, quite unconscious that he did so. 'And yet, I can't see such action doing much good. I can have all the suspicions in the world, but in this particular case the only thing that's going to do any good is proof.'

'Couldn't you get some?'

'Sufficient to show quite clearly that I'm not the murderer? I doubt it. It needs exceptional proof to prove a negative.'

'Then what, sir?'

'That was the starting point of this dismal conversation. What indeed?' He stood up. 'I'm going out for a walk.'

'Very good, sir.'

Verrell was that rare phenomenon, a man who liked walking for its own sake and not because there was no other form of conveyance immediately handy, and often when he wished to clear his mind he would leave his flat and cross into the Park and there spend a couple of hours strolling about.

The flower-beds were as immaculately kept as ever, and because of that looked vaguely unreal; two or three weeds amidst their geometrically exact rows would have introduced life. The grass was only moderately scarred from the depredations of those visitors who believed it to be their duty to destroy, and the trees were in full leaf, giving a pleasing mixture of various shades of greens.

He walked along the path, careless in which direction he went. When the end of the line was reached, where did one go? Knowing that the murderer had succeeded, what was there that he could do? Questions he had repeatedly asked himself since he had seen the paper; questions that permitted of no answers.

He admitted that there was no action he could take. How, then, was he to try and clear the name of Blackshirt? He laughed bitterly. Surely logic would force him to realize that the two problems were so integrated they were one and the same?

He had been walking for a long while, yet still his mind found it impossible to settle. He felt stifled. Had there been but one thing he could do he would have gained relief. But there was nothing.

For once he gained no pleasure from his walk.

*

Ashley had refused to take over the investigation of the Blair murder, yet he had insisted on pushing himself in on everything, and, in the eyes of others with especial reference to Traynor, making a thorough nuisance of himself.

It was Ashley who wanted to search for the place where the diamonds had been hidden. Traynor demanded to know why anyone should imagine there had ever been any diamonds within a couple of miles of the house, and Ashley's replies had been so evasive as to be downright ridiculous. The outcome of all this was that Ashley and Hooper had begun the search, and, after they had been at their task a considerable number of hours, their diligence was rewarded when they discovered that one of the castors on the larger of the two arm-chairs unscrewed, as did the metal plate to which it had been attached, and that beneath was a cavity about three inches deep.

'This is it,' said Ashley, and there was a minor note of triumph in his voice.

Traynor looked inside the space. 'The only thing that contains is air,' he muttered, illogically annoyed that the search had proved successful.

'Precautions as complex as this mean something valuable to conceal: the diamonds.'

'So maybe they were there; they aren't now.'

'No,' agreed Ashley slowly, 'but it's nice to have confirmation.'

'Some confirmation!'

Ashley leaned against the window, with his back to it. He stared at the chair. 'Dukes Blair must have hung on to them all this time, either waiting until he thought it was safe to pass them on, or else because he was keeping them as a reserve fund. The murderer came along, Dukes stood a hell of a lot of punishment, then couldn't take any more, and talked. The murderer found the diamonds, took them, killed Dukes.'

'Why do you keep using the word "murderer"—what's wrong with Blackshirt?'

He shook his head slowly. 'I wasn't really thinking.'

Traynor was curious. 'Where do you go from here?'

'I'd give much to know that one.'

'If Blackshirt has the lot, I suppose that's the last we hear of him?'

'For a while, yes. Until he feels like another little season of fun.'

Traynor rammed his fists deep down in his pockets. 'Next time he gets itchy feet I wish to hell he'd let them take him from my territory.'

'Having trouble?'

He laughed sarcastically. 'That's one way of describing the attitude of my seniors. The moment it became certain it was Blackshirt, they started tearing into me as though I'd asked him along as a personal favour.'

Ashley had not been listening to the answer to his question. He heaved himself away from the window, crossed to the door. 'Be seeing you.'

'O.K.'

Hooper joined the Superintendent at the head of the stairs, and together they descended. The front door was opened for them by a constable and they left the house, crossed to their car. The onlookers watched, fascinated.

The policemen returned to their office and, without being asked, Hooper prepared and served coffee.

'Thanks, Bill,' said Ashley. 'Need something to keep my thoughts away from the river and hundredweight bars of lead.'

'Things aren't that bad.'

'They're not exactly rollicking cheerful, are they? Blackshirt has grabbed the diamonds from Dukes Blair. That, as I've said before, seems to be that. In my humble opinion, we can kiss them and him good-bye, and if I'd any strength of character I'd go in and tell the A.C. so.'

'He'd really like that.'

'That's the way I think.'

'You know something: he'll come a cropper sooner or later.'

'The A.C.?'

'Blackshirt.'

'Why the hell should he? Been going for a long time now—and I'll bet you anything you like he suffers from the most depressing good health.'

They were silent, each saddened by his thoughts. The Superintendent handed over his cup. 'Give me another if you can squeeze the coffee-pot.' He waited until his cup was filled. 'They can chuck me out for saying this, Bill, but I wish Blackshirt had stuck to his old ways of life. There used to be a bit of fun in trying to nail him, but the way he acts now, the only thing one wants to do is squash him out of existence.'

'Fun for whom?' demanded the other sourly.

Ashley nodded his head. 'Not for the poor blokes trying to do the catching, I suppose,' he admitted.

*

Otto Speyer fiddled with the ivory paper-knife. 'I would have found him, given another twenty-four hours.'

'But you weren't,' said Blackshirt.

'I know.' He dropped the knife on to the desk. 'What I said must seem to you arrant nonsense, but it wasn't meant to be. I was trying to explain that I did my best for you, and that given time I should have succeeded.'

'I don't doubt it, Otto.'

'But I wasn't quick enough.'

'As you say.'

Speyer shifted uneasily in his seat. He had already let it be known the extent of his displeasure at the failure to carry out his orders. He knew his words would have brought fear. Now he himself was fearful. The cracksman was too contained: within him must be bitter fury. 'Is there anything else that can be done?' he hastened to ask.

'I doubt it.'

'He has all the diamonds now?'

'As I see it, yes.'

'He may try to sell through me, Blackshirt.'

'I shouldn't go nap on the possibility.'

'They could not be handled for a third time without my knowledge.'

'They will probably be taken abroad.'

Speyer picked up the knife and played with it once more. Never before had he heard a note of defeat in the other's voice. He looked up. 'There are still many, Blackshirt, who do not believe you committed the murders.'

'But very many more who do, no doubt.'

It was true. Success in others was not admired by the criminal fraternity, any more than in the rest of society. And in the case of Blackshirt, success had been going on for so long he was hated with vicious intensity. 'What do you intend to do now?'

'Try to tackle things from a different angle.'

'Will it do any good?'

'Who can say?' He laughed harshly, stood up, paced the floor, came to a halt. 'Have you heard nothing?'

'Nothing. Had I done so I should have told you.'

'This would be a good battle to win, Otto.'

The fence made no reply, but stood up and crossed to his cocktail cabinet which, day or night, had a near-hypnotic effect on him. He poured out two drinks, offered one to the cracksman. 'Up to now, you have never accepted. This is the time to break such rule.'

Blackshirt accepted the glass. 'Cheers.' He wondered ironically what people would say if they could witness the fence, noted for his harsh vindictiveness, trying to cheer up the one man he had cause to fear.

'Is there anything I can do?' asked Otto.

'Nothing.'

'Blackshirt. . . . It seems that the battle has been lost—are you not increasing the risks beyond all reason by carrying on?'

'Possibly.'

Speyer sighed. 'If I thought my words would have any effect I should continue, but it's like talking to a deaf mute.'

Blackshirt finished the drink, put down the glass on the desk.

'Another, Blackshirt?'

'No, thanks.' He walked towards the door, disappointed, although he had not seriously believed he would learn anything. Acknowledging his illogicality in no way made it less annoying. 'Be seeing you, Otto.'

'I hope so.'

Speyer watched Blackshirt pass through the doorway, close the door. He wondered if this were not the last adventure for the cracksman. The thought made the fence so sad he decided on another drink.

Chapter Eleven

COLONEL MONTGOMERY awoke, saw Blackshirt by the side of the bed, and decided instantly that never again would he ever accept an invitation from a Judge, be he even a Lord of Appeal in Ordinary. Since the day Parlant had been stupid enough to get his head bashed in—devil of a lot of fuss about that, too; in India, men were always getting their heads bashed in—there had been no peace for anyone, least of all Montgomery. Police inquiries, inquest and some damned coroner asking a lot of damn' fool questions, reporters, a visit, filled with insolence, from that blackguard Blackshirt . . . and now, when it had seemed as if all had at last been forgotten, here was the cracksman back again.

The colonel looked at the top drawer of his bedside table where was his revolver, remembered what had happened last time, lay still.

'Know anything about the present whereabouts of the Milton Cross diamonds?' asked Blackshirt.

'How dare you come back here!'

The cracksman calmly sat down on the side of the bed. Later, the colonel was to rip in half the top sheet in a ridiculous, but soul-pleasing, gesture of inspired hate.

'Last time I called on you, I wasn't certain what I sought. This time I am,' continued Blackshirt.

'I don't——'

'The Milton Cross was stolen by Albert Blair. When he was held, prior to the preliminary hearing of another matter, the Cross was stolen from him and the stones were divided between three people, two of whom have since been murdered. I'm looking for the murderer and the diamonds.'

The Colonel listened, but understood less than half of what was being said. This half, however, was sufficient to enable him to understand that his integrity was being called into doubt by a man who was a self-confessed criminal. The thought angered him intensely, and only a strong flow of words afforded him any relief.

Blackshirt listened and was impressed, and at the same time became convinced that the colonel knew nothing. That had always been his belief.

The murderer was a man with brains, and Montgomery would never have risen to so high a rank in the army if he had suffered from such defect.

The cracksman stood up. 'Sorry to disturb you—hope you'll soon get back to sleep.'

'Not until I've telephoned the police and told them precisely what I think of them for allowing a murderous blackguard like you to run loose.' The value of his words was lost because, as he realized when he had finished, Blackshirt had left the room at some early stage of the peroration.

He lifted the telephone receiver. It would not be his fault if the police did not become aware of what he thought about things.

*

Edward Fisher gathered himself up, then dived beneath the bedclothes. Not until in this latter position did he realize that he had left his wife to her fate and that bedclothes would hardly grant him any form of defence. His correct summing-up of the situation was high-lighted when his wife screamed and the blankets and sheet were forcibly removed from above him.

His wife screamed for a second time, and Blackshirt turned and was about to approach the other bed to try to calm the lady when she took matters into her own hands and fainted. The cracksman was not sorry.

'For God's sake, don't kill me,' groaned the unfortunate Fisher, still tightly curled up in his position of hiding.

'I've no intention of doing so.'

'I'll give you all I've got. . . . Don't kill me like you killed the others.'

'I've killed no one.'

'Don't kill me,' repeated Fisher, in no state to carry on an intelligent conversation.

Fisher's wife groaned, indicating her return to the conscious world. Blackshirt thought she would probably faint again and did not bother to take any further steps to keep her silent. He sat down on Fisher's bed. 'What do you know about the Milton diamonds?'

'I don't know anything about anything.'

'Take things more slowly.'

Fisher wondered what he had done in the past to deserve such brutal treatment at the hands of fate. 'What . . . what diamonds?' he asked.

'The Milton Cross—remember that?'

'Yes.'

'It was stolen by Albert Blair, who in turn, had it stolen from him. The diamonds are worth a fortune. Do you know where they are?'

'No . . . of course not.'

'You don't collect jewellery?'

'My wife has a little. . . . But it's all at the bank.'

Blackshirt allowed that to go unchallenged. He had searched the house before he awoke Fisher and had found a locked drawer in which were a few rings and one string of cultured pearls. He hoped Mrs. Fisher *did* keep her jewellery at the bank.

He asked a few more questions, left.

After a while Fisher looked down at himself because he was cold, and was surprised to find that he was still minus the bedclothes. He leaned down and pulled them up and over himself, and as he did so, his very active imagination presented him with a picture of what might have happened. Fear flooded through him, and for a while he was a little uncertain as to whether or not he had actually suffered such brutalities.

'Edward . . . Edward . . . Where are you?'

He remembered he had a wife, and glanced towards her. The quick look told him all, and he knew there was only one course open to him. Hurriedly he left his bed, and only dire necessity overcame the dread fear that the cracksman was lurking, waiting to pounce. Bravely, he carried on until he reached the brandy that was kept for emergencies.

It was only after partaking several remedial drinks that Fisher remembered his duty as a citizen. He telephoned the police, and although the man to whom he spoke was too polite to say so, the policeman was greatly surprised by the jovial tones of one who had been so lately visited by Blackshirt.

*

Panton's studio flat was without its owner but still housed the paintings. Blackshirt wondered whether the absence of the owner was permanent or temporary, checked. Clothes hung in the cupboard, books lay around the rooms, and a circular letter declaiming the virtues of a certain soap product was propped up on the small wardrobe. But tooth-brush, soap and hairbrushes were missing, there was no fresh food in the larder, and a layer of dust had settled in both the bath and the hand-basin.

He inspected the paintings once again and wondered what style they represented. One or two of them sported a title, but this, he found, only made matters the more confusing. Perhaps the only thing about them he really understood was the signature of the artist, and he found it slightly out of keeping that Panton should own and sign so ordinary a name. He was about to walk away when he suddenly had an idea and looked around to try and find something that would remove paint. In one corner of the studio was a table covered with the paraphernalia of painting, and Blackshirt tried the contents of the bottles, one after the other. At the fourth attempt he was successful, and as he stroked the canvas with the piece of soaked cloth, the rather cramped signature of Panton slowly vanished. In its place appeared another.

Blackshirt sighed. Information that came too late was worse than no information.

*

'Order more ice,' snapped Superintendent Ashley.

That the request was not intended to be carried out literally was clear.

Hooper contented himself with pouring out more coffee instead. 'Roll on my holidays.'

'Holidays! Ha!' Ashley drank half of the contents of his cup, lit a cigarette, and smoked it more or less normally. He tilted himself back in the chair until it was on two legs, rested his own legs on the desk. 'You'll be lucky, chum, if they give you off the Christmas after next.'

'My missus is threatening to go on strike—says she only sees me long enough each day to tell me there's been a call ordering me out again.'

'If that's all she says to you, you're lucky.' Ashley rounded his lips to enable him to blow smoke rings. He blew four times with complete lack of success, gave it up, exhaled smoke normally, and, much to his mortification, blew a perfect ring. He thought it summed up life.

'Why?' said Hooper suddenly. 'Why does he have to start up the whole thing again?'

'Because he reckons he hasn't caused us enough trouble, thinks we ought to be kept on our toes.'

'I'm beginning to wonder if that is the whole story?'

'You leave that sort of thinking to other people.'

'Blackshirt has been asking them if they know the whereabouts of the Milton diamonds.'

'I know what you're going to say. What he's just done makes it sound as though he doesn't know where the diamonds are now, that therefore it was not he who stole them, and, ergo, it was not he who did the killings. . . . Imagine you're Blackshirt, Bill. You've bumped off half the population and you've recovered the diamonds, so everything in the garden should be lovely, but it just so happens it isn't. You've had the misfortune to earn yourself the title of murderer, and being a sensitive sort of a gent, you want to get rid of it. How do you go about the job? You do precisely what Blackshirt has done—make it look to others as though you're still at the beginning post.'

'Just suppose it isn't that way, that he hasn't recovered the jewels but someone else has—what Blackshirt is doing now is what the old style Blackshirt would have done.'

Ashley laughed shortly. 'You're the one who jeered at me because originally I thought Blackshirt might not be the murderer—remember?'

Hooper checked to see if there were any more coffee in the pot, sadly found there was not. Since there was little hope his senior would offer him a cigarette, he lit one of his own. 'Bloke can change his mind,' he muttered.

'And I've changed mine, for good and all. Blackshirt is a murderer, and until he's brought in, no man, woman, or child in this country is safe from the depredations of this brutal killer.'

'You sound like Simpson.'

Ashley suddenly remembered that it had been Simpson, the Assistant Commissioner, who first spoke those stirring words. He felt aggrieved and angry that Hooper should have had the impudence to point out such fact. 'Whoever the hell said it, it's a fact.'

'You know something? Because we've concentrated on Blackshirt, we've tended to overlook a thing or two.'

'I'll lend you a pipe and deerstalker hat any time.'

Hooper remained silent. When Ashley was in a mood such as at present enveloped him he was liable to say things that in a more cheerful moment he would not. Hooper amended his thoughts. Ashley was ill-mannered at all times.

*

The two constables who watched Johnson's house called themselves the forgotten brigade. Each night they reported for duty, each night they were detailed to their present job because orders had come from high up that it should be so. The fact that everybody at the local police station was convinced the order would have been rescinded days before, if the same high-ups had remembered it, was neither here nor there. The Inspector was a man who regarded orders as sacrosanct.

'Not so warm tonight,' said Dean.

'Perishing cold,' muttered Talbot, who had taken over from Constable Seeton and regretted the change ever since. Man was made to sleep at night, not maintain a ridiculous and useless watch.

'Won't do my tomatoes much good.'

'Won't do us much good,' retorted Talbot, who loathed gardening and personal discomfort.

'I've planted some sweet corn this year; interested to see the result. Never tried it before.'

'Haven't you?'

'You need green fingers with that stuff, and no mistake.'

'Green fingers, my foot,' snapped Talbot. 'Shove the things in and leave 'em be; that's the way to make anything grow. All this fancy talk is a lot of rubbish.'

'Listen to the expert!'

'I know this much—it's a darned sight cheaper in the end to buy from the shops.' Having delivered which insulting remark, Talbot marched away from their improvised guard box and walked back along the grass verge, glad to move his legs. 'Green fingers,' he said aloud, in derisory tones of voice. 'Some of them couldn't make an overdraft grow.'

As he finished speaking he heard a sound from behind him. He turned. The night was darkish, but the new moon reflected sufficient light for him to make out the figure clothed in black. His brain recorded complete astonishment that trouble had come to them after all, then something crashed down on the side of his neck and the world spun away into complete and utter nothingness.

Dean heard the noise and judged that Talbot had fallen over something. It was just punishment for a man who could treat the sacred subject of gardening as did the other, but once that punishment had been administered it was time to forgive. Dean walked forward. 'What's happened?' he asked.

There was no reply.

'Where are you, mate?'

Dean was country born, had lived in it all his life. As with all true countrymen, he had frequently spent part of a night in chase of other people's pheasants and rabbits. He had excellent hearing, and immediately the sound occurred to his left he identified it as man-made, swung round, switched on his torch. The figure in black was harshly outlined, raised hand ready to bring the small cosh smashing down.

Dean, shrugging aside the initial shock, reacted quickly. He raised his left hand to ward off the coming blow, used his right to direct the torch immediately at the other in an effort to blind him. The cosh landed on the constable's forearm and the pain was immediate and intense. He groaned, dropped the torch, lashed out with his right hand. The blow was not accurate, and his fist skimmed the other's hooded cheek. Dean saw the cosh come down towards him again, then that was the last thing his mind recorded.

The man in black waited to note if any alarm had been raised. Satisfied it had not, he took from his pocket a roll of sticking plaster and with it secured the arms and legs of the unconscious constable.

He advanced quickly towards the house. He was in a hurry to settle a debt.

*

Dean regained consciousness and tried to move his arms. At the same moment as he became aware of the extent of his headache, he also realized that his limbs were tied. He began to struggle, but the effort intensified the pain in his head and he was forced to cease. Seven men with seven hammers, all striking the inside of his head at the same time, could not have produced the pain he experienced. It started at the back of his eyeballs, crossed the top of his head, spread out and down his neck. He wished the man in black had used a gun and had killed. It would have prevented the pain.

Some time later he overcame the pain sufficiently to think, and knew he had to break free. The resolution was arrived at with difficulty, but the effort involved was nothing compared to the task of carrying it out. Each time he strained at the bonds the pain increased alarmingly in his head, and each time he failed to free himself his fevered brain told him all his efforts would forever be a waste of time. . . . But a man who had once lifted two cock pheasants out of a tree that grew within ten yards of the head keeper's house was not one to give in easily. Each time the agony became too great he desisted, then, when he regained strength and resolution, he tried again.

Time had no meaning, so he had no knowledge how long it took him to break free, but the eastern sky was greying and stars of the smaller magnitudes were lost when he at last managed to strip off the tape from about his wrists, then from his legs.

He stood up, leaned against a tree for support. He touched the top of his head and encountered a bump great both for size and tenderness. He groaned. Never again would he leave off his helmet just because there was no sergeant about.

Dean would have given much to be allowed to retire to bed and blessed sleep, but a sense of duty proved greater than such desires. He went in search of Talbot and found him, struggling feebly, on a patch of long grass. He freed him, realized the other was severely injured, let him lie where he was, turned and made his way to the house.

He rang the front door bell several times and there was no answer. He walked round to the back door and again met nothing but silence. Desperate measures needed desperate remedies, and ignoring all teachings, he broke a pane of glass in one of the french windows, passed his hand through the space, and unlocked the catch.

He stepped inside the house, paused to let the pain in his head die down. About to use the telephone that stood on the small writing table, he checked his movements, decided he should very quickly search the house first.

He found Johnson in a bedroom. The man was dead, and like Parlant had not found death easily.

Dean turned and walked back to the door, sick in the stomach that any man could have been used in such manner. He had left the room and was about to close the door after him, when he heard the sound. He turned, horrified, all but panicked.

Incredible as it might seem, Johnson was not dead, although he and death were locked in close embrace.

Dean raced down the stairs to the telephone, lifted the receiver and dialled nought. For a brief moment his own injuries were forgotten.

*

Verrell studied the news and it was as though he heard the dulled echo of the last nail being hammered home into his coffinlid.

Yet another victim tortured by the vicious cracksman, left for dead; a policeman on the danger list, another injured.

He stubbed out the cigarette in the ash-tray, and so hard did he press, the paper of the butt split and tobacco spilled out over his fingers.

Nothing could lessen the damning effect of this last attack. The constable had struggled with the man, identified him as Blackshirt. Against such evidence no one could doubt any longer.

Never had he felt so futilely enraged.

He began to pace the room, trying to assure himself that things were not quite so black as he knew them to be, but was too much of a realist not to admit the whole truth.

The position was hopeless, and there was absolutely no way in which he could try to——. Quite suddenly, he realized something. The attack on Johnson spoke of a different story. Obviously the murderer had not all the diamonds, or there would have been no need to torture the unfortunate man. Yet why did he not have them? He must, according to all that had happened, have secured those of Brindle and Dukes Blair, and it seemed more than reasonable to suppose he had bought Johnson's. Even if this latter assumption were not correct and, not being the buyer, he had gone to Johnson to discover what had happened to them, Johnson would have talked long before the threat of torture.

Verrell tried to reach a satisfactory answer to the questions the facts raised, but failed. Every suggestion held so many flaws it was worthless. A sense of exasperation filled him.

He switched his mind to another tack, one that had about it a grain of hope. If the murderer had not yet succeeded, Blackshirt was left with a chance to fight—if one could call it as high as a chance!

How was he to tackle the problem? Where was he to start? The news had been that Johnson was very severely injured but still alive. Here was the one man who would know what the murderer was after.

*

The hospital had, under the National Health, taken on a new lease of decay. Built for the poor in the days when poverty was a crime second only to patricide, its architecture more closely resembled a dirty prison than anything else, a likeness in no way diminished by the rules and regulations under which the patients suffered. It consisted of four main buildings joined to each other by fly-walks, a grim and squalid structure for the nurses, and, in direct contrast, a small huddle of newly-built huts that almost looked clean and which were used to house the forms with which the staff had to deal.

Doctors worked to the best of their ability, as did the nurses, but their efforts could not alter by one jot the abhorrence to everything by all who were forced to stay in the hospital, nor alter their bitter resentment of the archaic and punitive regulation which reduced visiting hours to one half hour each day.

Verrell parked the luxurious car he had "chosen" earlier on. He looked about him and wondered if any other country could so actively live in the past. He experienced a deep feeling of relief that he did not live in the district, and trusted the members of the Hospital Committee had the sense to be ill somewhere else.

He switched his attention to other matters. The task before him was formidable, to put things mildly. By making the attempt he was probably running his neck full tilt through a noose, but since there was one chance in a thousand he might succeed, he was willing to take the risk. . . . And because no one would be able to conceive he could be as stupidly daring as he was about to be, perhaps those odds might be said to be two in a thousand.

He wondered where Johnson would be. Thankfully knowing nothing about this hospital, he had no idea whether it had any private wards or not. If there were none, then his task would be infinitely more difficult. Probably so much so that even he would have to cry off.

He lifted the case from the back of the car, got out and walked towards the first of the buildings that contained the wards, drew level with it. On the two halves of the swing door on ground level was printed "Ward 1A." Near the door was an arrow that pointed up the stairs and indicated the way to Ward 1B.

He continued walking, reached the next block, discovered this housed 2A and 2B, and a little later, that the next building was 3A and 3B. Only one chance was left to him, and when he thought of what rested on that chance, even his nerves tightened.

The arrow pointing upstairs said "Private Wards."

He climbed the stairs that curved as they ascended, and when halfway up estimated he had as much cover as he was likely to gain. He opened his bag and took from it white surgeon's coat, gloves, mask and cap. As a disguise it was as effective as the Blackshirt clothes. He hoped that the autocratic powers wielded by surgeons would silence anyone who might query the sight of him as if garbed for the operating table.

He continued to mount the stairs, and within him was a hard knot of excitement. One word from some ever-suspicious Sister, and . . .

He reached the small landing. Before him were the doors that led into the private rooms, while to his left was the fly-walk that gave access to the third block. He moved forward, opened the swing door, passed through with all the nonchalance of one entitled to be doing precisely what he was doing.

There was a narrow corridor, with doors on either side of it. Coming towards him was a nurse with a tray on which were many surgical instruments, and halfway along the corridor sat a policeman wishing himself miles away from the world of the sick.

It was obvious from the presence of the policeman that he had guessed correctly. He walked along the corridor. The nurse studied him, showed a certain amount of interest, but no sudden and overwhelming curiosity. As she passed him, she half-smiled.

The policeman watched Verrell approach, hesitated, stood up as the other stopped before the door he guarded.

'Going in, sir?' he asked.

Verrell nodded.

The policeman opened the door, closed it behind Verrell, returned to the chair.

Verrell looked down at the bed. Much of Johnson's face was covered by bandages, but such part as was not, showed the ravages of pain. He lay, motionless, eyes closed. Verrell approached more closely and the eyes opened.

'How are you feeling?' he asked.

Johnson stared up at him. 'It hurts like hell,' he muttered, and his voice was barely audible.

Verrell wished the murderer could be made to suffer as had Johnson and others before him. He sat down in the chair. 'I expect the police will want to ask you a few more questions later on.'

'I've got nothing to tell them.'

'I wish you would help them—then they wouldn't worry you any more.'

'There's nothing to tell.'

'From the way you were treated, it's obvious the man who attacked you wanted to know something. Can't you tell them what that was?'

'I don't know.'

Verrell wondered what motivated the other. Was it fear for himself, for the consequences should he talk, or a mistaken belief in honour among thieves?

There was a knock at the door. Verrell turned round 'Come in.'

The constable half-entered the room. 'Superintendent's back, sir, would like a word with the patient if that's all right by you?'

'In a minute.'

'Very good, sir.' The constable withdrew, closed the door.

Grimly, Verrell thought that the arrival of the Superintendent at the same moment as he had chosen was the kind of luck that defied description.

He wondered how long he could be before he faced the man outside. Would the Superintendent, with developed sixth sense, have a hunch that all was not as it should be? Had he, even now, sent for someone who could check on the surgeon at the bedside of the patient, strangely dressed as though about to operate? Would face-mask inevitably suggest black hood? . . . It was one of Verrell's greatest assets that he could see all the dangers, evaluate them, then set them aside from his mind. He did that now, as he questioned Johnson again.

'Did you hear?'

'Yes.'

'He wants to question you.'

'I've nothing to tell.'

How was he to pierce such stubborn defence? He leaned forward, spoke quietly, but distinctly. 'Aren't you going to tell him about the Milton diamonds?'

Despite the pain that clawed his body, Johnson knew and suffered great fear. He pressed himself further back against the pillows.

'That's what he's after, isn't it?'

'How . . .?'

'But you haven't got them. You sold your share to a man in Denmark and used the money to retire from the police force and buy yourself your house.'

'How d'you know?' whispered Johnson.

'Remember the last time you refused to talk? I went to a lot of trouble breaking into other people's houses and there leaving large and varied clues, all of which would have incriminated you.'

'Blackshirt!' Terror became even greater.

'Start thinking, Johnson. If I were the man who'd done this to you last night I shouldn't be here wanting to know what I'd said to you. If I'd come, I'd have done so to kill. I am Blackshirt. The man who tortured you was not, even if he wore the clothes. I want to find him—Johnson. I've a large debt to pay, you've a larger one. Care to help me?'

'The police . . .?'

'Will not learn from me how you were mixed up in the Milton case.'

Something akin to relief momentarily eased out the lines on Johnson's face. 'Get the swine for me.'

'I'll make it a personal call.'

He spoke again, but his voice had become too weak to hear. Verrell leaned across until only inches away from the other's mouth.

'The thirteenth diamond is missing,' whispered Johnson. 'When the murderer tried to get it out of Dukes, he found Dukes hadn't got it. He came back to me, said I had it, wouldn't believe me when I told him I hadn't.'

'Who has it?'

'I don't know—I thought Dukes did.'

Verrell leaned back. Thirteen was proving as unlucky as reputation would have it. Dukes Blair had died because of it. Johnson was likely to do the same. Finally, either the murderer or Blackshirt would crash to disaster in search of it.

There came a further knock at the door, and the constable apologetically looked inside. He coughed. 'Sorry to trouble you, sir, but the Superintendent is wondering how much longer you'll be?'

'Tell him kindly to contain his patience until I've finished,' snapped Verrell.

The constable looked more cheerful. He was a man with a literal mind, and intended to relay the message precisely as given.

The door closed.

'Anything more you can tell me that might help?' Verrell asked Johnson.

'Nothing.'

'Then I'll leave you.'

He stood up. His mind shifted gear and he forgot the thirteenth diamond, concentrated on the more immediate problems.

He was in trouble, spelled in capitals. So far, his own incredible nerve had kept his head above water, but if he were to break free of those men who waited, he would need still greater nerve. Much depended on Johnson. If the latter, at the beginning of the interrogation, related all that had happened, Verrell would not have time to make his escape. If on the other hand, he . . .

He had the kind of mind that would follow a train of thought to its logical conclusion with bewildering speed. Trying to work out how he was to avoid a man in Johnson's weakened condition telling the police what had happened—when to speak too soon would be disaster, and to speak later would be nearly as bad—he suddenly realized what would happen if Johnson did quite the opposite to remaining silent. He mentally weighed up the mind of the murderer as far as he could judge it, estimated how the other would react.

'Johnson,' he said.

The sick man opened his eyes. For a brief second there was non-comprehension, then memory returned. 'Yes?'

'Will you do as I ask? It may lay hold of the murderer.'

'What d'you want me to do?'

'When the Superintendent comes in here, answer nothing, for five minutes, then tell him what has actually taken place.'

'Won't he . . .?'

'You were too ill to understand what questions I asked you.'

There was only the slightest hesitation before Johnson answered, 'I'll do it.'

'This time tomorrow there may be something of interest in the newspapers.'

'I hope I'm alive to read them.'

It seemed doubtful, thought Verrell. He turned, walked across to the door, gripped the handle. In the next minute or two he would need every ounce of insolent nerve and self-confidence he possessed. He opened the door.

Superintendent Ashley swung round and glared belligerently. He had been waiting a long time, and that had tried his temper; moreover, the wretched constable, lacking any sense of tact, had relayed a message that was hardly likely to increase Ashley's sense of joy towards the world. 'Is it, by any chance, all right at last?' he demanded sarcastically.

Verrell closed the door. He tried to gauge whether or not there was suspicion amongst those who stood about him.

'I've a great deal of work to do,' snapped Ashley, knowing quite well he must contain his temper, and therefore becoming very eager to lose it. 'May I go in and have a word with him?'

'He's a very sick man,' answered Verrell.

'I know that, but his evidence is vital to the case I'm conducting.'

'That is of secondary consideration.'

Ashley, who could never enter a hospital without mental and physical revulsion, felt a greater than ever dislike of doctors. 'I've got to see him.'

'Got to?' Verrell paused. 'Surely that's the wrong word to use?' he asked loftily.

Hooper looked away hurriedly, afraid his expression might be misunderstood.

'Does that mean I can't see him?' demanded Ashley, striving to retain some measure of politeness in his voice.

'Not necessarily—I merely wished to point out that in this instance your wishes are of no account, and it is mine that take complete precedence.'

The constable could not entirely contain his delight, and as a result received a look from the Superintendent that quickly dulled his pleasure.

Verrell, about to be carried away by the pleasure of the position, wisely determined to concentrate on the job in hand. 'You may go in, but on no account are you to tire him; is that clear?'

'Yes,' muttered Ashley.

Verrell turned, walked away. Instinct demanded that he quicken his pace, escape before the Superintendent realized the truth; yet he forced himself to walk slowly, almost ponderously, as might an eminent surgeon be expected to do.

'Funny him being all dressed up like that,' remarked the constable, when the white-coated figure was beyond hearing.

'There's nothing whatsoever funny about it, and I'll thank you to keep your observations to yourself,' snapped Ashley, and immediately felt much better. He led the way inside the room and Hooper followed him.

They stared at Johnson. Ashley hastened to speak, to divert interest away from the sight of so much pain.

'How's life?' he stupidly asked, in the tone of voice of the healthy unable to meet on level terms the sick.

Johnson seemed to smile, which was hardly the reaction they had expected.

'Can you speak?'

'Yes.'

'I want you to tell me all about the attack that was made on you. Did you see Blackshirt without his hood? What did Blackshirt want to find out from you?'

'Can't remember.'

'Come now, Johnson, you must be able to remember.'

The sick man closed his eyes. He was very tired, and knew he would need all his strength to help Blackshirt.

Ashley leaned closer to the man in the bed. 'Why did he torture you?'

There was no answer.

Hooper shrugged his shoulders, held his right thumb pointing to the ground.

'Johnson, was Blackshirt trying to trace the Milton diamonds?'

There was again no response.

A man in white coat opened the door and looked inside. 'Don't overdo it, will you?' he asked. 'Chap's in a pretty bad way.'

'No,' muttered Ashley.

'Couple of minutes more at the most.'

'All right.'

The door was closed behind the doctor. 'Why can't they perishing well mind their own business?' demanded the Superintendent, with complete disregard to the order of things. 'What the hell am I supposed to be able to do in two minutes?' He turned and spoke to Johnson again. 'You must know how vital the information is to us.'

Johnson opened his eyes. He judged the necessary time had elapsed. 'Know who it was?' he whispered.

'Which—who are you talking about?'

'The doctor.'

'Johnson, we're not allowed very long . . .'

'The one who was in here first—he was Blackshirt.'

'I don't care who——' With perfect timing, Ashley's voice came to a halt. He studied the words that had been spoken and immediate and complete disbelief was followed by furious denial. 'Don't be ridiculous, man.'

Johnson smiled, even as the pain settled about him more closely.

'What . . . what did he want?'

'To ask me about last night.'

The Superintendent was about to speak again when he noticed Hooper tapping his forehead with right index finger. Of course! It was stupid of him to have believed the words, knowing the state of the man who had made them. He paused, then stood up. It was clear that there was no further point in their staying.

The policemen left the building, walked towards the police car that waited for them.

'Blasted waste of time,' snapped Ashley disgustedly.

'Maybe we can get some sense from him later.'

'Doubt it.'

They both felt aggrieved. Perhaps it had not been very logical, but they had come with hopes they would learn the key to the affair; they had discovered nothing.

A constable stepped from the driver's seat, opened the back door of the car for them. At that moment a young man came up to them. '*Weekly Post*,' he hurriedly said, by way of introduction. 'We've just had a telephone call to say that Blackshirt's been here impersonating a doctor— is that right?'

Ashley spoke slowly, in case he used words policemen should not. 'I do not know from where you received your information, but it is completely incorrect.'

The reporter was not discouraged. 'Chap who 'phoned went on to say Blackshirt had even gone so far as to pinch the wallet from your coat.'

Nothing could have stopped the Superintendent reaching up to the inside pocket of his coat.

As they watched his face they knew his hand found nothing.

*

Where was the thirteenth diamond?

Verrell stared at the contents of his glass and knew that very shortly he was going to have to mix himself another drink.

Dukes Blair had left with it. That was according to Johnson, and Johnson had lost contact with the other as soon as Dukes left the room in which the division had taken place. Verrell studied the question from a slightly different angle. Johnson had never had it. Had he done so, he would have sold it with the other four, or had he kept the large one back, would have spoken when tortured. No man would have suffered such injuries for the sake of a diamond. . . . Yet, if that applied to Johnson, it must equally apply to Dukes Blair, since he too had suffered most damnably before he was killed—so much so he had revealed the hiding place for his jewels, which by the nature of things could not have included the thirteenth diamond. That left one person. Brindle. Brindle had not been tortured. Why not? Brindle had not dared to sell the jewels once greed had forced him to take possession of them. When the murderer had sought them from Brindle, the solicitor had been scared enough to disclose their hiding place at once. For that reason, death had come to him quickly.

Suppose Brindle had had the thirteenth diamond, then the situation was filled with irony. When faced by the murderer, he had claimed Dukes Blair had it, while confessing to the possession of the four smaller ones. The murderer had taken those four, killed Brindle, sought Dukes Blair, tortured to find the large one as well as the other four, failed, been left with only Johnson alive from whom to learn the truth.

All this was based on one assumption. Brindle had been wily enough to keep the large diamond and the four smaller ones separate. Only then could he have admitted to the one, retained the other.

If he were right, and Brindle had had the thirteenth diamond, where was it now? The four had almost certainly been kept in the house, because Brindle had been murdered quietly and without fuss, which meant the murderer had been easily satisfied. If the four had been there, then so had the fifth.

All this had suggested itself to him when he had been in the hospital, but since his thoughts there had been so hurried he had wanted to check at leisure. Now he had checked and reached the same answer.

Would the murderer react in pattern? Would vanity blind him to the fact that there might be a trap concealed?

Verrell laughed. Trap was a double-edged word: although it was he who had set it up, it was more than likely to be he, himself, who slipped into it and was caught.

He finished his drink, crossed to the cocktail cabinet and mixed himself another. 'Cheers and good luck,' he said to himself.

Impatiently he waited for Roberts to return with the newspapers. So easily could everything have gone wrong, so that there was no trap, or trap within a trap, he thought, not without delight at the complexity of the matter. He heard the front door click shut.

Roberts handed him the evening newspaper. Blackshirt was headline news again, and so was Superintendent Ashley.

The thing had started, and must now continue, unaided by anything but the reactions of those who participated. He was banking everything on what those reactions would be. His life, to be exact.

Chapter Twelve

THE telephone call was routed through to Superintendent Ashley, a soured gentleman who imagined everyone of his colleagues was laughing at him behind his back. He was, in all too many cases, quite correct.

Hooper answered the call, handed the receiver to the Superintendent. 'For you,' he muttered.

'Let's have it then. . . . Yes . . . Yes . . . What's that . . .? Here, hang on.' He listened for a while longer, then held the receiver away from himself and stared at it with a strange expression on his face.

'Been recommended for immediate promotion?' asked Hooper, with heavy humour.

'Bill—we may have got the break we wanted.'

Hooper was astonished by the excitement in the other's voice. 'What's up?'

'That was Mr. A. N. Onymous. Wanted to know if I were interested in capturing Blackshirt.'

'The hell he did.' Hooper became equally excited.

'Said he could tell me where the cracksman would be operating this evening.'

'Where?'

'He's not talking right now, but will give another buzz later. Wants us to stand by during the night.'

'Sounds more like a perishing practical joker,' muttered Hooper, spirits suddenly dampened by the request.

'Not this time, Bill. I'll take a bet on with you as to that.'

'Do you think it——' He was rudely interrupted.

'We'll stand by with a dozen or so men.' The Superintendent stood up from his desk, crossed to the window and looked below. 'We'll get him this time if I have to tear him apart with my own hands to do so,' he said slowly. 'We'll teach all the smart Alecs who've been so funny at our expense that they haven't been quite so humorous as they thought.'

'I don't like it.'

'You haven't liked anything from the day you first shook hands with yourself.'

Hooper ignored the rudeness. 'Look at it this way—in all the years that Blackshirt has been around there's never been anyone who could squeal on him. Blackshirt works on his own, so no one else knows what he's doing. Why should there so suddenly be a change? Who could have learned something about the man who walks by himself?'

'I don't know, and I don't care, and if you're going to be a Jeremiah, go and be it somewhere else.'

'You're the boss.'

'And don't you forget it.' He looked at his watch. 'Wouldn't be too early for coffee, would it?'

Hooper stood up. Early or no, it meant the same thing. He had to make coffee.

*

Verrell parked the car, switched off the engine, lit a cigarette. He thought it could so easily be the last one he enjoyed in freedom.

Had he guessed correctly? Had he allowed for every contingency? Was he a quixotic fool dangerously to imperil himself as he was about to, merely to save the name of Blackshirt, when, should he let matters rest, he could remain safe and free? Of course he was. He grinned sardonically. He had been one before, and, should the gods be munificiently generous to him tonight, he would, no doubt, be one again before he retired.

He looked at the clock in the dashboard of the car and noted it was two o'clock. It was time to move; the moment of no retreat.

He threw the cigarette stub out of the car, checked that the white scarf was tied neatly around his neck, stepped on to the pavement. He locked the door. He had no wish to have the car stolen before he returned it to where the rightful owner had left it.

He began to walk along the road. The houses on either side of him seemed to attain an air of menace, as though they were witnessing his passage that they might give evidence upon it. The street lighting narrowed to infinity, outlining the path that led to destruction. He grinned; nerves less certain than his might have suffered from the suggested symbolism. He shrugged aside the danger, revelled in the excitement.

He reached the end of the road, turned. Now he was probably being watched by the murderer. Perhaps he had miscalculated and was marked down for death by bullet or knife, to be left lying in the street, branded by the black shirt he wore under the scarf, the black hood and gloves in his pockets, the belt of tools about his waist.

Two houses to go. No explosion of light and sound, no smashing impact of leaden bullet; no knife delivered by practised hands, splitting flesh and muscle.

One house to go. There must be no quickening of pace, nothing to indicate a wish to escape from the danger area, because to the unsuspecting there was no danger.

Blackshirt reached the shadow of the tree that stood in front of Brindle's house and there waited. Each of his senses was at its highest pitch of awareness and he kept himself ready for whatever action might suddenly be required of him.

The silence remained absolute.

He stripped off the white scarf, donned hood and gloves.

He tried to analyse his feelings at the thought that for the first time in his career as a cracksman he believed that every one of his movements was being watched. He knew a mixture of emotions, the chief of which was hatred of the watcher. The murderer must be squashed out of existence—and only Blackshirt was in a position to try to do so.

He walked up to the house. Once entered, the future would become the present, then the past. He slipped back the catch of the window. So be it.

*

Ashley lay back in his chair, head resting on the wood, snoring. He had loosened his tie, undone the top button of his shirt. His coat was caught up at the back of his neck so that it hung down his chest as though too small for him.

Proper dandy, thought Hooper, resentfully. Being unable to sleep anywhere but in a bed, he found such casual rest a disgusting habit. He looked at his watch for the tenth time within the last hour and consigned Blackshirt and Ashley to the devil, careless as to the order in which they went.

The telephone rang. Ashley awoke with a loud grunt, reached out and took the receiver from its stand as the Detective-Sergeant dragged himself to his feet and crossed the room.

'Yes . . . Where? . . . I know it. Right.' Ashley slammed down the receiver. 'Brindle's house,' he said tersely.

'Was that the same chap who rang you earlier?'

'It was Father Christmas for all I care. Get things moving.' He buttoned up his shirt, tightened his tie. He ran his tongue round the inside of his mouth, shuddered at what he tasted.

Hooper, excited despite his professed scepticism, telephoned through to the men who waited below. Then he and Ashley left the room and rapidly made their way down the stairs.

As they stepped out of the main building, so the first police car rocked to a halt and a back door opened. They jumped inside, the car jerked forward.

Ashley lit a cigarette. He had not felt so nervously excited since the first time he had had to decide whether to make an arrest. Not for a minute did he believe the two telephone calls had been fakes. Someone with an old score to pay off had discovered what Blackshirt was about to do, had leapt at the opportunity to bring the cracksman's career to an end.

He studied the road ahead of the car.

'Get a move on,' he snapped.

The driver looked at his speedometer. 'Doing nearly fifty now, sir.'

'Then take the blasted handbrake off.'

The constable, a brilliant driver, decided his professional conduct had been called into dispute. He pressed down on the accelerator and the noise of the engine rose. Behind him the three following cars found difficulty in keeping station.

They came to a halt before the huge, ugly house.

The men had been exhaustively briefed as to their duties, and had been instructed in the consequences should they fail in them. Most did not need such spur: their desire to settle accounts with the cracksman ensured that they carried out their orders to the best of their ability.

They encircled the house, and by using portable lights made certain that no part of the garden was in shadow.

Ashley stared up at the house. He remembered how Blackshirt had broken out of it the last time it had been encircled by the police, knew that such disaster would not happen again. The men had been warned; they would accept no order given by someone unseen, would on no account leave their post. Nothing, not even a troupe of dancing girls, would distract their attention from the house they were guarding.

Ashley had the key to the front door since it had not, conveniently, yet been handed back to the executors of the estate. He unlocked the door, swung it open. Their portable lights flooded the gloomy hall, sent the darkness flying backwards.

'Let's get cracking,' muttered the Superintendent. His voice was hoarse.
They searched the house. They found no one.

They met at the foot of the over-ornate staircase.

'Well?' muttered Hooper.

The Superintendent shook his head slowly. Disappointment clawed deep within him.

*

The difficulties of finding a hiding-place had made Blackshirt believe the task to be impossible. The police would miss nowhere where a two-foot midget might conceal himself.

Then, when all but ready to admit defeat, he had remembered the large open cistern in the loft. He had seen it when previously he had searched the house, and had at the time remarked upon its gargantuan size—it was as though an army had to be watered.

Imagination of a strange kind would be needed to direct a search beneath the calm surface of a cistern. It was not from such waters one expected frogmen.

He had waited until he heard the police arrive, then had stripped and fitted his clothes into the water-tight bag and had unfolded the sheet of black and soaked it. He dropped the bag into the water, followed it as he heard the sounds of the search approach. The water was cold. Not all the resolution he summoned would convince him to the contrary.

He pulled the black cloth over himself, attached one end of the thin black rubber tubing above the level of the water, kept the other in his mouth, as he lowered his head.

He waited, covered by the black cloth, the water pressing down on him. If they found him, there could be no struggle.

Light filtered through to him. The searchers were in the attic. He looked through the water and could see his body, and it appeared to be infinitely white and infinitely huge. Could anyone avoid seeing it as he saw it?

The sound of footsteps was muffled and it was impossible to tell from how far away it came. One moment, he judged the sounds were retreating, the next, he thought they were alongside the tank, and the police had found where Blackshirt hid.

The light grew dimmer, sounds became much less frequent, then ceased at the same time as complete darkness returned.

He sat up, eager to enjoy a normal supply of fresh air. He begun to shiver and could not force his mind away from hot rum grogs.

He stepped out of the cistern, dried himself, took out his clothes from the bag and dressed.

All that had gone before had been risky; compared to what was to come it had been beginner's work.

He stayed in the attic until the search of the floor below had been completed, then, as the police descended, so did he. Thus, when they gathered at the front door, dispirited, angry, he waited at the head of the stairs that led down to the hall.

'Call it off,' ordered Ashley, voice indicative of the disappointment he felt.

Hooper stepped outside the house, identified himself in the light, called out an order to the men who encircled the building. Slowly, the policemen came to the front door, silent, suffering from exhausted minds caused by the nervous tension they had been under.

Ashley was the last to leave the house, and he locked the door behind him. He stood and stared at the men, did not see them. He wondered why the false telephone call had been made. Had it been nothing more than a joke, or was there more purpose than that to it? Had it been made by a genuine squealer, or had Blackshirt himself telephoned, activated by a sense of humour others found less amusing than did he?

From the right side of the house came the sound of smashing glass. The noise was so unexpected it left the police motionless in shocked surprise for a measure of time; then they regained their senses, and almost as one man, turned and faced the direction from which the sound had come.

They saw a figure, dressed in black, running across the lawn. At first they doubted that what they saw was there, being more willing to believe that a vision was bothering them because they had thought about the cracksman too intently and for too long.

Hooper was the first to shrug aside this strange sensation. 'Go get him,' he shouted.

Ashley watched the men begin to run forward. His mind was overloaded with questions. What could this mean? Why had Blackshirt broken cover when there was absolutely no need to do so?

As the cracksman vaulted the wooden fence he was also asking himself the last question. The running constables behind him had about them the quality of a racing doom.

He reached the front door of the house next to that of Brindle's, thrust the piece of mica into the lock. If the door were bolted or barred he had lost, without further argument. He had banked everything on the fact that, since the building had been converted into flats, the front door would be secured only by Yale-type lock.

The nearest constable was almost at the steps that led up to the door. His head was thrown back, and he was pumping his arms backwards and forwards.

The mica seemed to stick, and the tongue of the lock refused to pull back. A second's panic would have been fatal. Blackshirt acted as though he had the rest of the night in which to complete the task in hand. He withdrew the mica, inserted it again, twisted. The lock moved; he pushed the door open.

The nearest constable leapt up the stairs and joyously threw himself forward. His outstretched hands gripped the cracksman's right arm, and for one short moment he told himself the fight was over and Robin McDowall had done what the rest of the police force had ever failed to do. Then he was swung round and launched forward into space with an elliptical movement that finally brought him into sharp contact with three of his companions who had been closely following him. They all crashed to the ground, amidst a welter of arms and legs.

Hooper jumped over the complicated tangle of humans, would have trampled on them, if necessary. Behind him panted Ashley, then the remaining constables, all of whom had found sprinting rather beyond them.

The door of the house was still open. Hooper slammed it inwards against the wall with his shoulder, swung his torch round, saw the light switch, pressed it down. The hall became clearly illuminated; it was empty.

'Surround the house,' gasped Ashley, painfully aware of the poor athletic figure he presented, puffing and panting, sweating from so few yards of running.

The men took up station around the house, again used their torches to form a barrier of light.

Ashley led four men up the stairs. He knew he should ask himself what was the meaning of Blackshirt's actions, but refused to do so. Perhaps he was making a fool of himself—yet if he let Blackshirt run into this house and stay there unopposed he would be making a bigger one.

They reached the first floor. To their right was a door on which was a name-card listing a married couple. Ashley ignored it, continued up.

There was no name-card on the door on the second floor, but there was a calling-card. Caught between the door and the jamb was a small strip of black cloth.

Ashley pointed to the door, could not find the words to order them to break it down.

Hooper and two constables threw their combined weight against the door. It resisted them for a while, then crashed open. They ran into the room, swung their torches backwards and forwards. Inside all was emptiness. Neither furniture nor cracksman was present.

They heard a window being forced open in the room beyond the one in which they were, and they rushed forward. The intervening door was again locked, and once more they set themselves to the task of battering it down. From the men who ringed the house outside they faintly heard a sudden and confused shout.

The door gave way.

The bottom half of the far window had been raised, and on the sill knelt a figure in black. The light glinted on the knife in his right hand.

The two nearest constables ignored the danger, threw themselves at the murderer. One received a raking cut down his leg, but so great was his excitement his mind did not record the fact until later. The three of them collapsed to the ground in wild confusion. Hooper stood over them, waited until he could act, then wrapped his arms about the neck of the cracksman and gained an arm-lock that was a killer. The struggle was over.

Ashley stared at the cracksman, and slowly assured himself that it was true and that his eyes were not playing him false.

He advanced until he stood immediately in front of the cracksman. This was a moment that was unique; had never happened before, could never occur again. He hesitated, to savour success to the full, then could no longer control his impatience. He ripped away the hood.

Blackshirt had a small, sharply-angled face, in which the most noticeable feature was the eyes. These were flat-grey in colour, and expressed bitter hatred.

The cracksman twisted violently against his captors' restraint, only desisting when his arm was held at such an angle he had to quieten or suffer a broken limb.

'They can retire me tomorrow,' muttered Ashley, filled with awe.

'Under six feet,' commented Blackshirt sullenly.

It had happened! Yet Ashley still was not ready to swear that the truth could be believed.

Hooper had been studying the face of the captured man. 'We've met this Johnny before,' he suddenly said excitedly.

'Where?' asked Ashley.

'With a beard—under the name of Panton.'

'Bill,' he answered slowly, 'you're dead right.'

'Something more.'

'Give.'

'If his face were slightly different where that skin looks a bit peculiar, we might be staring straight at a man who died some time ago. Albert Blair.'

'You're getting too ruddy clever,' sneered Blair, desperately trying to cover up his chagrin at being caught, his fear because he had been.

'Albert Blair,' repeated Ashley. Blair was Blackshirt! Dead Blair.

Hooper began to search Blair's clothes, and when he patted the trousers' pockets exclaimed with pleasure, inserted his hand inside the right-hand pocket, and pulled from it a wash-leather bag. At this, Blair renewed his struggles, and only stopped when again he was threatened with a broken arm.

They watched as Hooper opened the bag and poured the contents of it into the palm of his hand. The light became reflected and refracted as the thirteen diamonds seemed to glow from inner fires.

'Got them!' remarked Ashley triumphantly.

'Bit late in the day,' snarled Blair.

'Better late than never.'

'You sound like Mother's Hour.'

Ashley smiled. Anyone could compare him to anything. He felt as though all the misfortune he had ever suffered had now been more than cancelled out.

He took the diamonds from Hooper, was fascinated by the thought that he held a fortune. Quickly he returned them to the bag, dropped the latter into his pocket. No man could judge for himself when fascination would turn to desire.

'Cart him off,' he ordered.

They dragged a swearing, struggling Blair from the room.

'Pinch me to make certain,' said Ashley, when only he and the sergeant were left.

Hooper leaned against the wall. 'I want to see the faces of all those back at HQ.—the ones who were so busy laughing at us.'

'Reckon we can laugh now.'

'Even old Simpson'll have to say something nice.'

'He won't like that, not after all those names he called us last time.'

'And what were they?' asked a new voice filled with interest.

Ashley felt as though he had been pinched—very hard.

Blackshirt stepped into the room.

The Superintendent looked across at Hooper, but the latter was in no better position to offer assistance.

'You secured Blair well and truly, I trust?' asked the cracksman.

'Who . . .?'

'Who am I? Blackshirt.'

'Then . . . then he wasn't the real Blackshirt?' Ashley's mind slowly began to reason once more.

'Does it look like it?'

Hooper knew he ought to offer token resistance.

'I don't want to hurt you again,' remarked Blackshirt kindly.

Hooper decided he had offered token resistance.

'The man you've had taken away,' said Blackshirt, 'is the murderer of Parlant and Brindle. I did not commit the murders, as I told you before.'

Ashley slowly nodded his head.

'He is a very clever man . . . who became just too clever when he determined to lay the blame for his killings on me.'

'Did you know who he was from the beginning?'

'He had to be one of the guests of Parlant, because I visited each of them in turn after Parlant's death, and it was from that time that the murderer posed as Blackshirt—although no report of my interview with these three appeared in any newspaper. The question as to which one, could not be answered until I uncovered the stakes. I learned these were the Milton diamonds. I remembered how accurately it had been made to appear that the burglary at Parlant's house was an outside job, and that immediately suggested the murderer was an expert cracksman. Connected with the diamonds, there was already such a person: Albert Blair. He was dead, but a burned-out car and a charred corpse have been wrongly identified before now.'

'The corpse that was found must have been subjected to close identification.'

Blackshirt shook his head. 'It would have seemed ninety-five per cent certain who was the dead man; consequently, the only proof that was sought was to turn those figures into one hundred.'

'But——?'

'Blair picks up a tramp, someone whose absence will be missed by no one, kills him, burns him, as Blair.

Ashley grunted.

'Look at it from another direction. Who's to suspect anything? But for my intervention, who would have realized that the motive for these murders was the Milton diamonds?'

'The police——' began the Superintendent stiffly.

'Would have got nowhere. Not because of incompetence, but because they couldn't resort to the kind of investigations I could.'

'You can say that again,' muttered Hooper.

Blackshirt grinned. 'As soon as I knew what was at stake, I could sit down and think. Someone was after the Milton diamonds, knew where they were. Who knew? Those who had them, and the person from whom they were stolen. This could mean thieves falling out, one of them wanting more than his fair share. But in direct negation to this the Judge had been tortured, yet the possessors of the diamonds must know Parlant had not got any. This left only Albert Blair as the murderer.'

'How come Blair went for Parlant?' asked Ashley.

'I think you'll find it was faulty reasoning. To the criminal, lawyers are lawyers, whichever branch of the profession they adorn; also, all lawyers are the biggest thieves unhung—in a perfectly honest kind of a way, it should be hastily added. Albert Blair knew Brindle was one of those who had stolen the diamonds from him. Brindle was a lawyer, working with Parlant, and Blair could not visualize their standards of honesty being uncorrelated. If one of them was a crook, so was the other—they worked together, didn't they? Hence the reason Albert Blair tackled Mr. Justice Parlant, from whom, of course, he learned nothing.'

'He's not far wrong,' muttered Hooper, referring to lawyers, with whom he had had many a painful moment when in the witness box.

'Blair's a thorough worker,' said Ashley.

'Very,' agreed Blackshirt. 'He set out to gain himself a new identity after his escape from prison, and did so, taking on the mantle of an artist. He bought several paintings, all in execrable taste, and placed on them his name—shows he had no sense of shame. He set about cultivating friendships, and at some stage made that of Parlant. No doubt, seeing what an opportunity it offered him, he wangled an invitation to the Judge's house, and there spent the nights searching the house for the diamonds. When he couldn't find them he decided to use persuasive force, and that, while in the house, because, as with the Milton Cross itself, he worked on the principle that the obvious is ignored. He made it appear entry had been forced into the Judge's house. Who then was seriously going to suspect the guests, who, were any one of them the murderer, would not kill while a guest because that would be too obvious?'

'What happened tonight?'

'I gambled everything on my estimation of Blair's character. He wanted to trap me, expose me, not so much because that would mean the murderer would no longer be sought, but because his ego demanded that he beat me. The thirteenth diamond was almost certainly in Brindle's house—Dukes Blair, a clever swindler on his own account, must, at some stage, have lost out to Brindle with regard to this—and I knew Albert Blair knew this, having learned it from Johnson. I estimated that if Albert Blair learned I had found out where the diamond was he would do everything possible to make certain my attempt to find it would end in disaster. It was for this reason I rather pulled your leg at the hospital.'

The Superintendent winced.

'I knew Brindle's house had two similar houses on either side converted into flats, and that one of these was to let. I put myself in Blair's position, wondered whether I would want to see the humiliation of my adversary, decided I should. I then told myself that I would watch such humiliation from this empty flat.'

'So you led the police from Brindle's house to this one,' murmured the Superintendent in some awe.

'Blair would not expect such a move—hence the way in which he was caught on the wrong foot.'

'You took one hell of a risk.'

'I did rather,' agreed the cracksman with classic understatement.

Ashley felt an unprofessional admiration for the other.

'Whereabouts did you hide in Brindle's house?' asked Hooper suddenly.

Blackshirt chuckled. 'I reckon we'll let that question slide; my hiding-place may come in handy some other time.'

Ashley coughed. Events had been proceeding as smoothly as a vicar's tea party, and it was time they could be likened more to a W.V.S. jumble sale.

'All in order?' asked the cracksman.

The Superintendent found himself nodding his head in the affirmative before he could stop himself.

'Good. Then if you'll walk into this cupboard I'll lock you in. You'll soon break free, but it'll give me time to get clear.'

They entered the cupboard because they were rightly convinced there was no alternative.

They waited until they judged all was clear, then they battered their way out of the cupboard. They looked at each other, said nothing. Probably there was nothing to say.

*

'Well?' demanded Simpson, the Assistant-Commissioner, angry at having missed so much sleep.

'We got one of them, sir.'

'What the devil are you talking about?'

Reluctantly Ashley explained.

'Rank stupidity to allow the real Blackshirt to escape,' muttered Simpson, but his next few words showed he was not really bitter. 'Still, we have recovered all the Milton diamonds and laid low Albert Blair for the last and final time.'

'We've done that, sir.'

'Let's see these famous diamonds that have caused all the trouble.'

Ashley took the leather bag from his pocket, handed it across to Simpson. The latter undid it, rolled the contents out on to the top of his desk. The diamonds reflected the light and seemed to turn it into abstract wealth.

He picked up the biggest one, fingered it, replaced it. 'Carbon,' he said, 'worth a king's ransom. Little bits of nothing equal to your and my salary for the next two hundred years. One, two, three . . .' He began to count, reached twelve and stopped. He looked up. 'I thought there were thirteen diamonds,' he snapped.

'There are, sir,' replied the Superintendent.

'Only twelve here now.'

'That's impossible; they must all be there.'

But they were not. Blackshirt had proved to be as avid a collector as ever of mementoes.

If you enjoyed *Double for Blackshirt*, please share your thoughts on Amazon by leaving a review.

For more free and discounted eBooks every week, sign up to our Endeavour Media newsletter.

Follow us on Twitter and Instagram.

35878347R00094

Printed in Poland
by Amazon Fulfillment
Poland Sp. z o.o., Wrocław